Shelby Young

An Original Screenplay
Written By
Kim Damiano

First Edition

Published by Damiano Publishing
 Damiano418@aol.com
 www.damianopublishing.com

Printed in the United States of America

ISBN: 0-9788268-0-9

For Mom, Dad, & Brian

FADE IN INT.---SAPELO HOSPITAL---
DAY.

At the end of a long corridor is the delivery room.

SUPERIMPOSE: August 13, 1974. Inside the delivery room, DR.ADAM MULCAHEY and three NURSES deliver the baby of CILLA YOUNG, 24. Cilla's mother, DAIVA YOUNG, 44, holds her hand. However, she is not particularly warm, rather she is firm, with a "just suck it up" attitude. CILLA looks extremely frightened by the whole experience.

                    DR. MULCAHEY
You're doing good, Cilla. Doing good. Can you give me another push?

CILLA shakes her head.

                    DAIVA
Come on, Cilla. Just push.

                    DR. MULCAHEY
Breathe, Cilla. Just a few more pushes and you'll be done. You can do it.

CILLA obliges.

                    DR. MULCAHEY
All right, I see the head. Come on, Cilla,

just a few more.

A NURSE wipes Cilla's head with a wet cloth. CILLA continues to push. She looks up at DAIVA, who's stare is serious and cold. CILLA gives another good push and finally, a cry from the new BABY can be heard.

DR. MULCAHEY hands the BABY to a NURSE, then he cuts the umbilical cord.

                    DR. MULCAHEY
                    (Genuine excitement)
You did it, Cilla! You have a new baby girl.

CILLA throws her head back against the pillow in exhaustion. DAIVA lets go of her hand. She watches as the NURSES clean up the BABY. CILLA closes her eyes.

DR. MULCAHEY removes his mask, revealing a big smile. NURSE CARTER walks towards him, carrying the BABY---all cleaned up and wrapped in a blanket.

                    DR. MULCAHEY
There she is.

CILLA opens her eyes. NURSE CARTER walks towards her.

                    DR. MULCAHEY
Say hello to your daughter, Cilla!

NURSE CARTER goes to hand the BABY
to CILLA, but CILLA shakes her head "no,"
and puts her hand up, shunning the baby.

                    CILLA

Hmm. Umm.

DAIVA sighs. NURSE CARTER is
stunned.

                    DR. MULCAHEY
                    (Whispers)
Maybe she's just tired.
                    (To CILLA)
We'll bring her back in a little later, after
you get some rest, ok?

CILLA doesn't reply. NURSE CARTER is
stunned. DR. MULCAHEY prompts her to
take the BABY out of the room. DAIVA
looks at CILLA, who is expressionless as
she watches NURSE CARTER take the
BABY out of the room.

                                        CUT TO:

INT.---NURSERY---NIGHT.

In the middle of the third row of
NEWBORNS, one BABY lies peacefully

sleeping, while the OTHERS around her squirm and cry. It is SHELBY YOUNG.

Standing outside the window, CILLA watches her daughter sleep. Again, she shows no emotion. No happiness; anger; regret; nothing.

CUT TO:

INT.---HOSPITAL ROOM---DAY.

CILLA sits up in the bed. Her packed suitcase sits at the end of the bed.

A new baby outfit is laid out on the dressing table. CILLA starts to walk out of the room just as DAIVA enters.

DAIVA

Where are you going?

CILLA

There's a new mother I've been talking to the past few days. I want to say goodbye to her.

DAIVA nods. CILLA walks out of the room, then she walks down the hallway. About half way down, she looks back, then proceeds to the exit.

CUT TO:

EXT.---SAPELO HOSPITAL---DAY.

CILLA steps out of the hospital and into a
waiting cab. Before she closes the door, she
looks up at the window of her hospital room.
Without remorse, she closes the door and
the cab drives away.

CUT TO:

INT.---HOSPITAL ROOM---DAY.

DAIVA paces the room, but she remains
reserved. She steps out the door and looks
down the hallway. She doesn't see CILLA
anywhere. NURSE CARTER walks
towards the room, carrying SHELBY. She
enters the room and is bewildered.

                    NURSE CARTER
Where's Cilla?

DAIVA shakes her head.

CUT TO:

INT.---HOSPITAL ROOM---DAY.

While DAIVA argues with the HEAD
NURSE, NURSE CARTER dresses
SHELBY in her new outfit. SHELBY
smiles and playfully kicks the entire time.

DAIVA (O.S.)
Well, you tell me how this happened! I can't believe you just let her walk out of here!

HEAD NURSE (O.S.)
Mrs. Young, I assure you we didn't just let her leave. She never signed any release papers or anything.

DAIVA (O.S.)
She just went down the hall…how could she just walk out?

Soon, the voices of DAIVA and HEAD NURSE fade into a jumble, as NURSE CARTER continues to dress SHELBY. She smiles with an air of sadness for the abandoned child.

CUT TO:

EXT.---YOUNG CAR---DAY.

SUPERIMPOSE: September, 1979.

DAIVA steps out of the car and walks around to the passenger side. She goes to open the door, but 5-year old SHELBY has already opened it and is climbing out of the car.

                    DAIVA
                    (Stern)
You got your book bag?

                    SHELBY
Yeah.

                    DAIVA
Yes.

                    SHELBY
Yes.

SHELBY clutches the vinyl bag that is
almost as large as she is, in one hand, and a
small stuffed rabbit in the other. She closes
the door and starts to walk towards the
Sapelo Elementary school, but DAIVA
stops her.

                    DAIVA
Shelby, give me your hand.

SHELBY stops and obliges. DAIVA takes a
firm grip of Shelby's hand and they walk at
a brisk pace.

                    DAIVA
You don't want to be late for your first day
of school, now.

DAIVA eyes the ragged rabbit.

                    DAIVA
You should have left Lenny in the car.
They're not going to let you take him with
you.

SHELBY doesn't respond. They finally
arrive at the door, where her teacher, BETH
CARNEY, awaits, greeting each new
kindergartener. BETH squats down so she
is eye level with SHELBY.

                    BETH
                 (Genuine)
Hi, Shelby! Mrs. Young.

                  SHELBY
Hi!

                    BETH
Are you all ready for your first day of
kindergarten?

SHELBY nods. DAIVA nudges her.

                  SHELBY
Yes, ma'am.

                    BETH
Who's your friend there?

She points to the rabbit.

                    SHELBY
Lenny.

                     BETH
Lenny.

                    DAIVA
She watches that program, "Laverne &
Shirley," with her cousin, so she named her
rabbit, Lenny. God knows why.

BETH smiles.

                     BETH
Shelby, why don't you let Lenny go home
with your Mama? He'll be waiting for you
when you get home, then you can tell him
all about your first day of school!

                    DAIVA
Oh, I'm not her Mama, I'm her
grandmother. Her Mama left her in the
hospital the day she was born and we
haven't seen or heard from her since. So,
Shelby lives with her grandpa and me.

BETH looks at DAIVA. She is taken aback
by her crassness. BETH looks at SHELBY,
who is unaffected.

BETH

Tell you what, just for today, why don't we
let Lenny see what it's like to be in
kindergarten, ok?

SHELBY
(Smiles)

He'll like it, I'm sure.

BETH

I hope you will too. Come on, Miss Shelby.

BETH stands up and extends her hand to
SHELBY, who grasps it firmly.

DAIVA

Now the bus will drop her off right in front
of our house, so she won't have to cross the
street, right?

BETH

Right. Twelve-thirty sharp.
(To SHELBY)
Say goodbye to your grand mom, Shelby.

SHELBY turns and waves goodbye.

SHELBY

Bye.

DAIVA

Behave yourself.

DAIVA watches as BETH leads SHELBY inside. She cracks a small smile, one that requires more effort to suppress than to just give in and smile.

CUT TO:

INT.---CLASSROOM---DAY

The TWENTY FOUR STUDENTS sit in groups of six, at four tables, as BETH walks around and hands out large sheets of blank paper.

BETH

Ok, kids, we have a half hour left before it's time to go home, so I want you all to draw a picture of your first day of kindergarten. There are boxes of crayons in the center of each table. Draw whatever you feel about your first day. You can draw something you did, or someone you've met, anything that will remind you of your first day of school. Take turns with the crayons. Share with your neighbors.

She hands SHELBY a piece of paper. The KIDS all grab for the crayons and eagerly start drawing. As they draw, most of the KIDS start chatting among themselves, but SHELBY is different. She is quiet and serious as she draws her memory of the day.

BETH

I want you to make a nice drawing, so when you go home, your mom or grandma can hang it up on the refrigerator or your dad or grand dad can hang it up in his office.

These words encourage SHELBY to strive for perfection with her drawing.

MONTAGE SEQUENCE: Shelby Drawing

SHELBY draws a square for a building, then she begins to draw little bricks inside the square.

SHELBY draws a big yellow sun.

SHELBY draws a side walk leading to the building.

CUT TO:

EXT.---YOUNG HOUSE---DAY.

DAIVA stands by the front door and waits for the school bus to arrive. Finally, the school bus pulls in front of the house and the bus door opens. SHELBY gets off the bus quickly. Her book bag is slung over her shoulder and she carries Lenny in one hand, and her drawing flaps in her other hand, as she runs to the front door.

                    DAIVA
How was school?

                    SHELBY
Good.

She hurries into the house, then into the
kitchen. She flings her book bag, then
Lenny, onto the kitchen table. She holds
onto her drawing.

DAIVA enters the kitchen. SHELBY shows
her the picture.

                    SHELBY
Look! We had to draw a picture of our first
day of school!

She hands DAIVA the drawing. She looks
at it, but she is indifferent.

                    SHELBY
Mrs. Carney said to hang it on the
'frigerator.

                    DAIVA
That's nice.

She sets it back on the table, then goes to the
counter to continue preparing sandwiches
for lunch.

DAIVA

Is that all you did at school? Draw?

SHELBY

No, we did more.

DAIVA

Go put Lenny and your book bag away, and
wash up your hands for lunch. You can tell
me about it then.

SHELBY looks at DAIVA, then at the
picture sitting on the table. She picks up the
picture, as well as Lenny and her book bag,
then she walks to her room.

CUT TO:

INT.---SHELBY'S ROOM---DAY.

SHELBY plops her book bag on the floor,
then plops Lenny onto her bed, then she
walks to her desk. She gets a piece of tape,
then walks over to a bare space on her wall.
She hangs the picture up on the wall. In the
drawing, Shelby is standing before the
building; Shelby is drawn very tall and the
school building is drawn very small. The
stick-figure Shelby towers over the building-
--confident and a little defiant. After she
hangs, the drawing, she bounds out of her
room.

EXT.---SCHOOLYARD---DAY.

It is recess. The CHILDREN run around the playground. A group of about ten play on the merry-go-round. The boys pushing the girls, then vice versa.

SHELBY stands off to the side and just watches the CHILDREN playing on the merry-go-round. She is not sad or lonely, rather she is observant. She watches all the action going on around her; the merry-go-round; two GIRLS jumping rope; a group of BOYS playing with a nerf football. She also notices a lone boy, PALMER RYCE, sitting on the ground, leaning against the school building. She watches him intently.

CUT TO:

EXT.---SCHOOLYARD---DAY.

PALMER RYCE sits on the ground and cries. He buries his face in his hands, but it is still obvious that he is crying. SHELBY walks up to him.

SHELBY
Why are you crying?

He looks up, kind of embarrassed.

PALMER

Because I can't tie my shoe.

SHELBY looks down and sees his shoe is untied.

SHELBY

Sure you can.

PALMER

I can't! I tried three times and I can't.

SHELBY

Well, try four times then!

PALMER

I can't.

PALMER buries his face in his hands again.

SHELBY

Want me to show you?

He looks up and nods.

PALMER

Ok.

SHELBY squats down.

SHELBY

First, you pull your tongue.

PALMER gives her a funny look, then pulls his tongue out of his mouth.

SHELBY laughs.

SHELBY
Your shoe tongue! Your shoe has a tongue, right here, and you pull it. Like this.

She proceeds to pull the tongue of his shoe. As she tells him how to tie his shoe, she does it step by step for him.

SHELBY
Then you pull the laces real tight and cross them over like this. Then you go under with this one and pull them to the side. Then you make a loop like this and pull this side around the loop and then pull and you get another loop and then you're done. See?

PALMER admires his newly tied shoe.

PALMER
Thank you.
SHELBY
You're welcome.

SHELBY then unties his shoe.

PALMER
What, what are you doing!?

SHELBY

Now you're going to do it!

PALMER

I can't!

SHELBY

Yes, you can! Just do what I did.

SHELBY guides him and together, they tie
his shoe.

SHELBY

See, you did it!

PALMER smiles.

PALMER

Wanna, wanna, wanna p-p-play tic-tac-toe?

SHELBY

Sure.

PALMER stands up and pulls a piece of
chalk out of his pocket. He and SHELBY
sit down on the ground, and he draws a tic-
tac-toe board, on the cement.

PALMER

You, you, you can go first!

He hands SHELBY the piece of chalk. She
draws a big "X" in the center square, then

21

hands PALMER the chalk. He draws an
"O" in the top right hand corner. SHELBY
draws an "X" in the top left corner.
PALMER immediately draws an "O" below
his other "O." SHELBY quickly draws an
"X" in the bottom right corner and draws a
line through her "X's."

                    PALMER
                    (Dejected)
Aww. Wanna, wanna play again?

                    SHELBY
Sure!

PALMER draws another tic-tac-toe board.
He hands SHELBY the chalk again.

                    PALMER
Winner goes first.

SHELBY draws an "X" in the top left
corner this time. PALMER draws an "O" in
the center. SHELBY draws an "X" next to
her other "X." PALMER draws an "O" next
to the center "O." SHELBY puts an "X" at
the end of her row, to win the game again.

                    PALMER
                    (Amazed)
Man, you're good!

SHELBY smiles.

                    SHELBY
Let's play again.

                    PALMER
Ok!

This time SHELBY draws the board and
draws an "X" in the center square.
PALMER draws an "O" in the bottom left
corner. SHELBY draws an "X" in the
bottom right corner.

PALMER studies the board, then draws an
"O" above his other "O," leaving the space
open for SHELBY to win the game.
SHELBY looks at the space, but opts to put
her "X" in the space below the center.
PALMER smiles when he sees the open
space, then he draws an "O" in the top
corner, for the win.

                    SHELBY
You won!

PALMER smiles. He draws another board,
and they start a new game.

                    DISSOLVE TO:

INT.---SHELBY'S BEDROOM---NIGHT.

SHELBY lies on her floor and draws a
picture of her and Palmer playing tic-tac-toe.
They are drawn equally proportionate.

MONTAGE: Palmer & Shelby

Hundreds of school KIDS run around the playground, throwing balls, jumping rope, or playing on the merry-go-round. However, two CHILDREN sit alone and separate from the others; SHELBY and PALMER sit on the steps of the school and draw pictures in a sketch pad.

There is a thunderstorm outside of the school. Inside, SHELBY, who is visibly scared by the storm, sits next to PALMER, who holds her hand.

SHELBY and PALMER play tic-tac-toe on the playground.

SHELBY anxiously stands and looks out of the screen door. She bounces from side to side until she sees PALMER walk sheepishly into the yard. He is disheveled as he always is. SHELBY smiles and runs outside to greet her friend. He smiles. SHELBY immediately starts talking to him as she leads him into the house.

SHELBY and PALMER sit on the living room floor and play with Shelby's "square people" toys. DAIVA watches from the kitchen and cracks a small smile that only lasts for a moment, then she goes back to preparing her meatloaf.

In class, SHELBY draws a picture of
PALMER, as he sits drawing.

SHELBY walks into her room. She has just
gotten home from school. She sets her book
bag down, then immediately retrieves her
drawing of Palmer from her bag. She walks
over to her desk and picks up her eighteen
page thick scrapbook that she has created by
stapling all of her drawings together. She
adds the drawing of Palmer to the
scrapbook.

                                    FADE OUT:

FADE IN---EXT.----STREET LEADING
TO THE YOUNG HOUSE---DAY.

SUPERIMPOSE: "SUMMER, 1983"

SHELBY, now 8, and PERCY ELLISON,
her 12-year old cousin, walk down the
street, towards the house. PERCY wears a
baseball glove and tosses a softball into the
air and catches it as they walk. SHELBY
dutifully carries Percy's baseball bat.

                    PERCY
I wish the coach would let me play
shortstop. I wouldn't have missed any of
those balls, would I, Shelby?

SHELBY

Not a one.

PERCY

Darn right about that. (pause) Oh well, maybe next game. (pause) I hit good, though, today. Had two singles and a double. Woulda' had a triple but my asthma started up.

They walk on in silence a little ways, before PERCY speaks again.

PERCY

When is that little friend of yours coming back from vacation?

SHELBY

Friday!

PERCY

When he comes home, you going to stop coming to my games?

SHELBY

No way! He'll come with me!

PERCY

Good, because I always hit better when you're there, Shelby Sue. You're my good luck charm.

                    SHELBY
What's a good luck charm?

                    PERCY
It's something that brings you luck. For
some people it's an object, like a lucky
bracelet or cross, or a teddy bear or a lucky
t-shirt. For me, it's you.

                    SHELBY
I don't have one of those.

They approach the house.

                    PERCY
Well, we'll have to find you one, then,
won't we?

                    SHELBY
Sure.

                                        CUT TO:

INT.---YOUNG HOUSE---DAY.

BERNICE ELLISON, 35, Percy's mother
sits in the living room watching the
"Guiding Light" soap opera. PERCY and
SHELBY enter the house.

                    BERNICE
Hey, sweetie! Hey, Shelby. How'd you
do, Perc?

PERCY

We won, twelve to nothing! We crushed
them! I had two singles and a double.

SHELBY

Would have been a triple, but her asthma
stopped her.

PERCY

It slowed me down, Shelby, it didn't stop
me!
(Boisterous)
Nothing can stop Percy Elizabeth Ellison!

BERNICE

I can, Miss Percy. You and Miss Shelby
both need to get washed up and clean up all
y'all's toys before your grandma and
grandpa get back from the market.

PERCY

Yes, ma'am.

SHELBY follows PERCY down the hall.

CUT TO:

INT.---YOUNG LIVING ROOM---NIGHT.

DAIVA and HANSON YOUNG, her
husband, sit on the couch and watch TV.
DAIVA knits while she watches. BERNICE
sits in the recliner and watches TV.

SHELBY and PERCY sit on the floor and play Monopoly. SHELBY rolls the dice, then moves her car game piece down the board.

SHELBY

Virginia Ave.

She looks at her cards.

SHELBY

I already own that. Your turn.

PERCY rolls the dice and moves her shoe game piece down the board.

PERCY

Community chest.

PERCY draws a yellow card and reads it.

PERCY

Congratulations! You are a winner in a beauty contest. Collect $10 from every player. Hand it over, Shelby Sue!

SHELBY hands PERCY the money, then quickly rolls the dice. As she moves her game piece, PERCY watches the TV. "Happy Days" has just ended.

PERCY

Ooh, Shelby, it's almost time!

SHELBY looks at the TV and immediately gets up. PERCY gets up too, then they both walk into the hallway. DAIVA just shakes her head. HANSON, bewildered, looks at them.

They hook arms and wait at the edge of the hall.

PERCY
Ready.

The opening theme song to "Laverne & Shirley" comes on, and SHELBY and PERCY enact the famous "Shle meel, shle mazel" step like Laverne & Shirley.

PERCY & SHELBY
1,2,3,4,5,6,7,8. Shle meel, shle mazel, has enfefer incorporated!

They run in place, burst out in laughter, then fall to the ground.

BERNICE laughs. HANSON is slightly amused.

HANSON
You two are nutty!

BERNICE
Oh, Daddy, they're just having fun!

HANSON

That's all right.

PERCY & SHELBY
(Sing loud and bad)

…And we'll do it our way, yes our way, make all our dreams come true, for me and you!

They settle down, sit and continue to play Monopoly.

PERCY

I love this show, but it's not the same without Shirley.

SHELBY

Laverne doesn't need Shirley anymore. She's tough.

PERCY

Never thought of it like that.

DAIVA notices a car pull up in front of the house and stop. DAIVA watches as a WOMAN, steps out of the car, then pulls out a suitcase. The WOMAN closes the car door, then the car drives away. DAIVA watches as the WOMAN approaches the front door, which is open. The screen door is closed. Finally, the WOMAN, arrives at the door and knocks. DAIVA gets up and wallks to the door.

                    DAIVA
My word.

The woman at the door is CILLA.

HANSON, BERNICE, PERCY, and
SHELBY all look at the door. DAIVA
answers it, and CILLA walks in.

                    CILLA
Hello, Mama.

                    DAIVA
Cilla.

HANSON and BERNICE are surprised.
PERCY and SHELBY don't know any
better.

                    CILLA
Daddy. Bernice.

                    BERNICE
Cilla.

SHELBY is immediately taken by the
mysterious woman.

                    CILLA
I was just passing through town and I need a
place to crash for the night. I didn't think
you would mind.

HANSON

Of course not.

All stand in awkward silence.

CILLA

If you all don't mind, I'm kind of tired. We can talk in the morning, if you'd like.

Without waiting for an answer or acknowledgement, CILLA proceeds down the hall. Shelby is still mesmerized by her.

SHELBY

Who is that?

PERCY

I don't know.

BERNICE and HANSON look at DAIVA.

DAIVA

That's one of my other daughters, Shelby. She's your Aunt Cilla.

PERCY shrugs and goes back to the game. SHELBY continues with the game too, but she takes another look down the hall.

CUT TO:

INT.---YOUNG HALLWAY---DAY.

PERCY steps out of her bedroom and walks towards the kitchen. She stops at the end of the hall when she hears DAIVA and CILLA talking. She remains in the hall and listens.

DAIVA (O.S.)
So, why are you here now? It's been eight years, Cilla!

CUT TO:

INT.---YOUNG KITCHEN---DAY.

DAIVA and CILLA sit opposite one another at the kitchen table.

CILLA
Things didn't work out so well in California, so I'm going to Nashville. Like I said last night, I'm just passing through.

DAIVA
Eight years, Cilla, without not so much as a letter or a phone call. You could have been dead for all we knew!

CILLA
Well, I'm not dead, Mama. I'm alive and I'm well and I'm just passing through.

DAIVA
So you've said. (pause) What about Shelby?

CILLA

What about her?

DAIVA

Well, are you going to tell her that you're
her Mama?

CUT TO:

PERCY. She is shocked.

CUT TO:

CILLA stands up and walks to the sink.

CILLA

Oh, Mama, why would I do that? There's a
reason why I left her all those years ago. I
wasn't ready to be a Mama then, and I sure
as hell ain't ready now.

DAIVA

When will you be ready?

CILLA

I don't know. Probably never. What she
doesn't know ain't going to hurt her none.

DAIVA

What you did to me and to that little girl
wasn't fair, Cilla.

CILLA

What's fair Mama? I didn't want no baby. I
have dreams, Mama! Why should I ruin the
rest of my life for one stupid night I spent
with Clinton Davis?

DAIVA

What about my life? I've already raised my
children---

CILLA

Mama, I don't want to talk about this.

DAIVA

You think you can just show up here, after
eight years, and act like nothing happened,
like their ain't nothing wrong?

CILLA

I'll be gone by tomorrow morning, Mama,
then y'all can go back to forgetting about
me like you've been doing.

CILLA walks away, but DAIVA isn't
finished.

DAIVA

Don't you even want to know what I told
her?

CILLA stops, but doesn't turn around to
face DAIVA.

CILLA

I'm going to take a shower, Mama. I'll be
out of your hair tomorrow.

With that, CILLA walks towards the hall,
where PERCY remains standing. CILLA
passes her, but doesn't say anything.
PERCY condemns her with her eyes as she
walks away.

CUT TO:

INT.---YOUNG KITCHEN---DAY.

SHELBY sits at the kitchen table. Her
scrapbook lies on the table next to her cereal
bowl. PERCY pours the milk into her bowl.

PERCY

Move your book, Shelby Sue. You don't
want to ruin it.

SHELBY slides the book over. She glances
into the living room, which is empty.
PERCY pours herself some cereal and milk,
then sits down opposite SHELBY.

SHELBY

Where's Aunt Cilla?

PERCY

Who cares? What are we doing today,
Shelby Sue?

SHELBY shrugs.

                    PERCY
We could go down to the quarry or we could
go fishin'.

                    SHELBY
Fishing!

                    PERCY
Ok.

SHELBY looks back at the empty living
room. PERCY notices. Both girls eat their
cereal in silence.

                                        CUT TO:

INT.---BERNICE'S BEDROOM---DAY.

PERCY helps BERNICE make her queen
size bed.

                    PERCY
Mama, I heard them talking this morning. I
know that Cilla is Shelby's mama!

                    BERNICE
That is none of your business, young lady.

                    PERCY
It is my business, Mama. Shelby is my
family. She deserves to know the truth!

BERNICE

That is not your place to say or your
decision to make. Your Aunt Cilla has to do
what she has to do.

PERCY

So you think it's ok what she did?

BERNICE

No, I don't think it's ok. I would never
leave my child, Percy. You are my life!
Cilla's always been different. She always
marched to her own drum, was always
carefree. I knew when she got pregnant she
wasn't going to be all right. She wasn't
going to be in that child's life very long.
And just 'cause she's older, doesn't mean
that's going to change. It's best if Shelby
goes on thinking that Cilla is just her aunt.

PERCY

Well, I just think it's the biggest kind of sin
to lie to that child about her Mama!

BERNICE

And who are you, missy, to judge? You're
still wearin' pig tails and blue jeans!

PERCY

Yeah, well I know what's right, Mama, and
there ain't nothing right about what you'all
are doing to Shelby. Nothing.

CUT TO:

EXT.---POND---DAY.

The Sapelo Lighthouse can be seen off in
the distance.

SHELBY and PERCY are fishing in a small,
aluminum boat. PERCY props up her rod,
then pulls out a small bag of Hanson's
chewing tobacco from her pocket. She
opens the pouch, pinches some chew
between her thumb and forefinger, then
drops it into her mouth like she's been
chewing all her life.

                    PERCY
Want some?

                    SHELBY
Yeah.

PERCY pinches a small amount of chew,
then drops it into Shelby's open mouth.
PERCY puts the chew away, then picks up
her rod. Both girls sit patiently, waiting for
the fish. After a moment, SHELBY speaks.

                    SHELBY
How come you and Aunt Bernice live with
Grandma and Grandpa?

                    PERCY
Well, when I was a little girl, my Dad was a
soldier and he died fighting in the Vietnam

war. I was only five years old when he died. I hardly knew him. I can still remember his face, but his voice--- I can't recall anymore the sound of his voice. Anyway, me and Mama lived with Grandma and Grandpa ever since.

                    SHELBY
Does Aunt Cilla have any kids?

PERCY is quiet for a moment, while she ponders how to answer the question.

                    PERCY
No, she doesn't. She's never around any place long enough, I guess. (pause) No ma'am she doesn't have any kids and that's her misfortune. So it's just me and you, Shelby Sue!

                    SHELBY
                    (Smiles)
That's all we need!

                    PERCY
Right on, Shelby! Right on!

                                        CUT TO:

EXT.---YOUNG PORCH---NIGHT.

CILLA sits on the porch and smokes a cigarette. HANSON walks out onto the

porch, then sits beside CILLA. HANSON
hands CILLA an envelope full of money.

                    HANSON
I know this is why you are here, Cilla. I
don't want you to have to ask for it.

                     CILLA
Why are you giving this to me?

                    HANSON
Because you're my daughter, and I love you
no matter what you have done.

CILLA takes the envelope, then hugs
HANSON. He closes his eyes and squeezes
CILLA tight. He has missed his daughter.

                                        CUT TO:

INT.---YOUNG LIVING ROOM---NIGHT.

SHELBY walks into the living room,
carrying her scrapbook. CILLA sits on the
couch and talks on the phone. SHELBY sits
on the couch next to CILLA and opens her
scrapbook. CILLA pays no attention.

                     CILLA
                  (To Phone)
Charlie, it's Cil. I got waylaid here in
Sapelo, but I'm leaving in the morning.
Probably be there by evening. (pause) Yeah.

(pause) Yeah. I miss you too, baby, but I'll be there soon. (pause) Yeah. My love to ya. (pause) Ok bye.

CILLA hangs up the phone.

                    SHELBY
You're leaving tomorrow, Aunt Cilla?

                    CILLA
Yeah.

CILLA looks at SHELBY, but is uncomfortable. She quickly gets up and heads for the hall. She stops, then turns to SHELBY.

                    CILLA
Goodnight.

                    SHELBY
Goodnight, Aunt.

CILLA sighs, then proceeds to her room. She closes the door behind her, ponders for a moment, then begins to pack up her suitcase.

                                        CUT TO:

INT.---YOUNG HOUSE---DAY.

CILLA grabs her suitcase and walks out of

her room, closing the door behind her. She walks down the hall through the empty house, then out the front door. A cab is waiting for her at the end of the drive. She walks down the steps without ever noticing SHELBY, who sits on the front porch swing, her sketch pad on her lap, as always.

                    SHELBY
Bye.

CILLA stops and looks at her. She just offers a quick wave, walks down the drive, then gets into the cab.

SHELBY watches the cab drive away. She is reflective for a moment, but then she sees PALMER shuffling down the street.

SHELBY smiles.

                    SHELBY
Palmer!

She drops the sketch pad on the floor, jumps off the swing and runs to the end of the drive way. PALMER offers a lop-sided grin, as his friend approaches.

                    PALMER
Hi, Sh-sh-sh-Shelby!

Finally, she meets him at the end of the

driveway.

SHELBY

How was your trip?

PALMER

It was fun! New-new-new York is n-n-neat!
We saw two big buildings, they were both
the same, but one had, one had, one had a b-
b-big antenna on the t-t-top! And-and-and I
went to the top of the 'pire State Building,
and saw the Yankees play baseball!

SHELBY

Wow, you did a lot.

PALMER

Yeah, but I'm going back there pretty soon.

SHELBY

Oh, yeah.

PALMER

Yeah, I'm, I'm going to live there.

SHELBY is stunned. Her joy at seeing her
friend again, melts into sadness.

CUT TO:

EXT.---YOUNG BACKYARD---DAY

SHELBY and PALMER sit on the swings,
but they don't swing. PALMER looks at the

45

ground, as he twists his swing. SHELBY
sits, stoic, as she slowly rocks her swing
back and forth.

PALMER

I don't want to live in New York, Shelby.

SHELBY

I don't want you to either. (pause) When
are you going there?

PALMER

Soon, s-s-so I can s-s-start school. What,
what, what if they don't like me there,
Shelby.

SHELBY

Oh, they'll like you, Palmer. I like you!

PALMER

I'm scared to move, but my dad said I could
have my own room and, and, and, that New
York has a really big apple there…

SHELBY laughs.

PALMER

Wha-wha-what's so f-f-funny?

SHELBY

New York is the big apple! It doesn't have
a big apple!

46

PALMER

Oh.

He is embarrassed, but he laughs. SHELBY
laughs too, until both are overcome with the
giggles.

DISSOLVE TO:

EXT.---PALMER'S HOUSE---DAY.

SHELBY stands at the end of Palmer's
driveway, and watches as the moving truck
is loaded up with the Ryce's furniture.

DISSOLVE TO:

EXT.---PALMER'S HOUSE---DAY.

The last moving truck pulls out of the
driveway and drives away. The RYCE
FAMILY pulls out of the driveway. As they
do, PALMER looks out the window and
waves goodbye to SHELBY, who stands at
the end of the driveway. PALMER and
SHELBY keep waiving until the car
disappears on the horizon. Tears streak
Shelby's face. PERCY and DAIVA walk up
behind her. PERCY nudges SHELBY, who
turns around and sobs. PERCY grabs
SHELBY and gives her a long, supportive
hug, as she cries. After a moment, DAIVA
breaks up them up.

                    DAIVA
Come on, girls. It's time for dinner.

With that, SHELBY, PERCY, and DAIVA
walk towards their house. PERCY wraps
her arm around SHELBY as they walk.

                                        CUT TO:

INT.---SAPELO ELEMENTARY SCHOOL
CLASSROOM---NIGHT.

MRS. BYRNE sits at her desk. The
classroom is decorated for Halloween. It is
parent's night at the school. MRS. BYRNE
makes some notes in a student's file, then
she looks up to see DAIVA walking into the
classroom, towards the desk. She stands up
and greets DAIVA.

                    MRS. BYRNE
Mrs. Young, pleasure to meet you.

                    DAIVA
Likewise, Mrs. Byrne.

                    MRS. BYRNE
Please, have a seat.

DAIVA sits down.

                                        CUT TO:

INT.---SAPELO ELEMENTARY SCHOOL
CLASSROOM---NIGHT.

MRS. BYRNE discusses Shelby's report
card with DAIVA.

                    MRS. BYRNE
As you can see by her grades, Shelby is an
exemplary student. She's very studious and
takes her studies seriously. She excels at art
and spelling, and I feel she is most
enthusiastic about her artwork. She's a very
gifted child. She's a very polite and well
behaved young lady. But, I've been
concerned about Shelby this year.

                    DAIVA
                    (Surprised)
How so?

                    MRS. BYRNE
Well, she's very much on her own, kind of a
loner. I never see her interacting with other
children at recess, or when we have free
time. She spends most of her time drawing.

                    DAIVA
That's all she does at home, too.

                    MRS. BYRNE
I'm not saying that's bad, but Shelby needs
to develop her personal relationships a little
better.

DAIVA

She's nine years old, Mrs. Byrne.

MRS. BYRNE

I know, but since her friend moved away, she hasn't even tried to fit in with the other kids. That could become a problem down the road.

DAIVA

Well, I don't see any problem where Shelby is concerned. Her grades are good, she's not a problem child.

MRS. BYRNE

No, but there is more to life than good grades, Mrs. Young, even for a nine year old---especially for a nine year old. Shelby needs to start developing social skills now, or like I said, there will be problems in the future.

DAIVA sighs and purses her lips.

CUT TO:

INT.---YOUNG KITCHEN---DAY.

SHELBY and PERCY sit at the kitchen table. SHELBY draws a picture, while PERCY works on her math homework.

PERCY

I don't know why I have to take math. It's
not going to do me any good down the road,
so why bother, right?

SHELBY

Whatever you say, Perc.

PERCY

You're such a nut! You get straight A's all
the time! I'm going to be an actress or a
professional ball player, so I don't need
math!

SHELBY

But if you play ball, you have to know your
average.

PERCY

See there you go again, being all smart!

PERCY shakes her head in jest.

DAIVA walks into the room.

DAIVA

Percy, can I talk with Shelby for awhile,
please?

PERCY

Sure thing, G-ma! I need a break from these
numbers.

PERCY gets up, picks up her apple off of the table, then leaves the room. DAIVA sits down next to SHELBY. SHELBY just continues to draw as DAIVA talks.

                    DAIVA
Your teacher says you're having a hard time making friends. Is that true?

                    SHELBY
Hmm. Umm.

                    DAIVA
Excuse me?

                    SHELBY
No. She's wrong.

                    DAIVA
Do you have any friends at school?

                    SHELBY
Palmer's my friend.

                    DAIVA
You should have made new friends by now. Palmer's not coming back.

SHELBY stops drawing and looks at DAIVA for the first time, only for a moment, then she continue to draw.

DAIVA

You can make new friends, can't you?

SHELBY

I don't need any friends.

DAIVA

Really? How's that?

SHELBY shrugs.

SHELBY

I don't know. I just don't.

DAIVA

Aren't you lonely?

SHELBY

No.

DAIVA sighs.

DAIVA

You girls clean off this table, so I can get
dinner ready.

SHELBY

Yes, Ma'am.

DAIVA gets up and walks away. SHELBY
continues her drawing; It is a drawing of her
sitting on a swing. Next to her is an empty
swing.

INT.---SHELBY'S ROOM---NIGHT.

SHELBY places the drawing into a new scrapbook that she has started. Four scrapbooks now sit on her desk.

CUT TO:

EXT.---YOUNG HOUSE---DAY.

To establish. SUPERIMPOSE: SPRING, 1986

PERCY stands by the front door, impatiently throwing a softball into her mitt, over and over again.

                    PERCY
Shelby! Hurry up! I'm going to miss batting practice!

CUT TO:

INT.---YOUNG HOUSE---DAY.

SHELBY lumbers out of her room, carrying her sketchpad. She walks into the living room, where CILLA is sleeping on the couch. SHELBY takes a long look at her, before she walks out the door.

EXT.---BASEBALL DIAMOND---DAY.

SHELBY sits in the stands and draws as she watches PERCY pitch. PERCY throws a strike.

                    SHELBY
Nice pitch! Keep it up, Percy!

SHELBY continues to draw.

PERCY throws another pitch, but this time the BATTER hits the ball deep into center field. It falls for a hit. PERCY jumps up and points at second base as the BATTER heads for second.

                    PERCY
Go to second! Go to second!

SHELBY watches as the BATTER makes it safely into second base.

                    SHELBY
Come on, Percy! Shake it off!

SHELBY goes back to her drawing. PERCY pitches. This time, the BATTER hits a ground ball just to Percy's left. She dives, stops the ball, then from the ground, throws the BATTER out at first. She pumps her fist.

                    PERCY
Yeah!

SHELBY stands and claps, then sits back
down and goes back to her drawing, as
PERCY and TEAM run off the field, to their
bench. This whole time, it is implied that
Shelby has been drawing the game. Instead,
she is drawing, in perfect detail, a picture of
Cilla sleeping on the couch.

                              CUT TO:

INT.---YOUNG HOUSE---NIGHT.

SHELBY puts the drawing of Cilla into her
scrapbook, which along with her drawings
have become more sophisticated.

                  DAIVA (O.S.)
Shelby! Come and set the table!

                    SHELBY
Coming.

SHELBY closes the scrapbook, tucks it
under her arm, then walks into the living
room. She sets the book down on the coffee
table, across from where CILLA sits and
talks on the phone.

CILLA

Uh-huh. Uh-huh. (pause) I---I don't know
anymore, Donny. I just ---it just isn't
working out for me…huh? (pause) I don't
know. Maybe a day or two.

CILLA pays neither SHELBY nor the
scrapbook any attention. SHELBY
proceeds to the kitchen.

CUT TO:

INT.---YOUNG KITCHEN---NIGHT.

The YOUNG FAMILY sits and eats dinner
in awkward silence. HANSON and DAIVA
sit on opposite ends of the table, with
SHELBY and BERNICE on one side, and
PERCY and CILLA on the other. They eat
pork roast, corn and rice. CILLA doesn't
look anyone in the eyes. HANSON just
concentrates on his food, as does BERNICE.
Occasionally, PERCY will glance at
SHELBY, who sneaks an occasional peak at
CILLA. DAIVA, eats very little, as she
focuses her harsh stare at CILLA.

Finally, SHELBY breaks the silence.

SHELBY

Aunt Cilla, you can have my bed tonight so
you don't have to sleep on the couch again.

PERCY, BERNICE and DAIVA look at
CILLA for her response.

CILLA
(Sheepish)
Thank you, Shelby, for the offer, but I'm not
going to be in Sapelo much longer. The
couch suits me just fine.

SHELBY
(Nods)
Ok.

BERNICE
That was nice of you to offer, Shelby.

SHELBY offers BERNICE a slight grin,
then ALL go back to silent eating, until
PERCY speaks.

PERCY
Mama, me and Twyla are going out to the
Dairy Queen after dinner, if that's ok with
you?

BERNICE
That's fine with me, sweetie. Shelby going
with you?

PERCY
Ah, sure.

BERNICE nods. PERCY kicks SHELBY

under the table.

SHELBY
(On cue)
I don't much feel like ice cream tonight.

BERNICE
Why not? You sick or something?

SHELBY
No. Just don't feel like it.

BERNICE
All right.

CILLA looks at SHELBY.

CILLA
I'm not feeling much hungry myself tonight.

DAIVA
Feeling guilty, are you?

CILLA
Now for what on earth would I be feeling
guilty for, Mama?

PERCY
(Instinctive)
You know what, Shel, why don't you come
with me? I got to leave now.

CILLA

No, you know what, I'll be leaving. The
air's a little stifling in here. Always was.

With that, CILLA gets up and walks outside.
DAIVA doesn't react. BERNICE and
PERCY relax. SHELBY just continues to
eat.

HANSON
(To DAIVA)
Get me some more pork roast, please.

DAIVA shoots him a look, then gets up.

CUT TO:

INT.---SHELBY'S ROOM---NIGHT.

SHELBY lies on the floor and draws.
PERCY pops into the room.

PERCY
Hey, me and Rodney are meeting out at the
lighthouse. You gonna cover for me?

SHELBY
You and Twyla are at the Dairy Queen.

PERCY
(Smiles)
You're all right, Shelby Sue!

SHELBY
(Disinterested)
Uh-huh.

PERCY
You'll understand in about four years!

SHELBY
Have fun.

PERCY
I intend to! Goodnight!

SHELBY
'Night.

PERCY leaves and SHELBY continues to draw. She draws CILLA sitting at the dinner table eating. The drawing captures the essence of Cilla; confused, uncomfortable, selfish.

CUT TO:

EXT.---YOUNG PORCH---NIGHT.

CILLA sits on the porch swing and smokes.

DAIVA comes outside and sits beside CILLA.

DAIVA
This can't keep happening, Cilla.

CILLA

Mama, don't start---

DAIVA

Don't you interrupt me. I mean it. Now,
unless you want to take responsibility for
that child in there, I don't want to see you
here again, ever.

CILLA looks at DAIVA, then turns away
and takes a drag on her cigarette.

DAIVA

Don't you ever ask yourself what you are
doing with your life? What a waste it's
been? Where you off to now, Cilla? Huh?
Pretty soon you're going to run out of places
and men to run to! Here, you've got a
special, beautiful daughter sitting inside.
Aren't you even one bit curious about her?
Don't you want to know anything about her?
Don't you want to know that she hates
broccoli, but she loves brussel sprouts; that
she gets A's in everything except for math;
that she's had the chicken pox, but never
strep throat; that she's mesmerized by
lightning but hides when she hears the
thunder? Does any of that matter to you?

CILLA
(Fierce)

No it doesn't! Not one damn bit does it
matter to me, Mama. Yeah, I gave birth to

that child, but she isn't mine! And I don't want to know anything about her. I made my decision years ago and lived with it, so why can't you? Shelby has. She doesn't need me, she's doing just fine.

DAIVA
How do you know what she needs---

CILLA
I just know!

DAIVA
And what about you, Cilla? What do you need? What is it that you keep searching for that you ain't finding?

CILLA is reflective.

CILLA
I don't need anything and I don't need anyone, Mama. (pause) I will pack my things and be gone in the morning. You won't have to see me ever again.

DAIVA
Maybe not, but I have to live with your mistake everyday.

CILLA goes back into the house. DAIVA, stoic as usual, remains sitting on the porch swing. A low rumble of THUNDER can be heard.

CUT TO:

INT.---SHELBY'S ROOM---NIGHT.

A THUNDERSTORM rages outside. A
loud clap of thunder wakes SHELBY, who
sits up, startled. She reaches for her stuffed
rabbit, Lenny, then gets out of bed.

CUT TO:

INT.---YOUNG LIVING ROOM---NIGHT.

CILLA sits up on the couch and watches the
storm. SHELBY walks into the room.

                    SHELBY
Did the thunder wake you too?

                    CILLA
No. Just can't sleep.

                    SHELBY
When it storms, I come and sit in here 'til it
passes. Usually, there's no one here. Just
me.

                    CILLA
Well, by all means, don't let me stop you.
Sit.

Shelby sits on the couch. She sits sideways,
so she can watch the lightning out the

window. CILLA notices.

CILLA

Lightning is fascinating, isn't it?

SHELBY

Yeah.

CILLA

All that energy…and it's got anywhere in that big old sky to go.

Another loud clap of thunder rattles SHELBY.

CILLA

Thunder, however, is a different story.

SHELBY

I don't really like the thunder.

CILLA

The thunder is just making way for the lightning, just letting everybody know that the lightning is coming through.

SHELBY

The lightning really doesn't need the thunder to do that.

CILLA

No, it doesn't. Lightning can stand on it's own just fine, and it does. It always will.

SHELBY gets up and kneels on the couch to look directly out the window. CILLA turns more towards the window and they both watch the storm.

DISSOLVE TO:

INT.---YOUNG LIVING ROOM---NIGHT.

The storm has ended. Only a light rain falls and an occasional, silent lightning flashes. SHELBY dozes off. CILLA wakes her.

CILLA
Shelby. Shelby, why don't you go on to bed? The storm is over.

SHELBY, half awake, gets up and walks to her bed.

SHELBY
Goodnight, Aunt.

CILLA
Goodnight, Shelby.

CILLA watches as SHELBY shuffles down the hall. CILLA wearily wipes her face with her hand. She is startled by PERCY, who is soaking wet, sneaking into the front door. PERCY is equally startled to see CILLA awake.

                    CILLA
Meeting a boy at the lighthouse, huh?

PERCY doesn't know what to say.

                    CILLA
I only know that 'cause when I was your
age, I used to do the same thing.

Without a word, PERCY proceeds to her
room. CILLA looks out the window as a
brief lightning flashes across the sky.

                                        CUT TO:

INT.---YOUNG HOUSE---DAY.

CILLA stands by the door, watching. A
TAXI pulls up in front of the house. CILLA
picks up her bag. She pulls a sealed
envelope out of the outside pocket of the
bag. "Shelby" is written across the front of
the envelope. CILLA sets it down on the
table, then she steps outside the door. After
a moment, she comes back inside, grabs the
envelope, tears it up, shoves the remains into
her bag, leaves the house, then gets into the
taxi.

                                        CUT TO:

INT.---SAPELO MIDDLE SCHOOL---
DAY.

SHELBY sits in her art class. She is working on a drawing of her and Percy fishing in their small boat. Her drawings have become more detailed and sophisticated. The teacher, MRS. SHAW, walks around to each student and looks at their work, commenting on each one. She walks over to Shelby's table, and starts with the BOY at the end, eventually making her way to SHELBY.

MRS. SHAW
That's good, Roger. Much improved. Denton, you're getting better.

She arrives at SHELBY. She is very impressed.

MRS. SHAW
Wow. Shelby, that is really good.

SHELBY
Thanks.

MRS. SHAW leans over and studies the drawing.
MRS. SHAW
This is fantastic, Shelby. Look at the detail!

MRS. SHAW picks up the drawing to examine it further.

MRS. SHAW

Very nice.

She moves on and SHELBY goes back to work.

INT.---SAPELO MIDDLE SCHOOL
CLASSROOM---DAY.

One by one, the STUDENTS turn in their drawings to MRS. SHAW. SHELBY is the last to turn hers in.

MRS. SHAW

Shelby, I want to talk to you for a minute.

SHELBY

Yes, Ma'am.

MRS. SHAW

I really think this drawing is phenomenal. You are a very talented artist, Shelby. I want to enter this in the Sapelo community art show.

SHELBY
(Surprised)

Really?

MRS. SHAW

Yeah! I think you've got a real shot at

winning a ribbon for it. (pause) Don't you think this is good?

                    SHELBY
It's ok.

                    MRS. SHAW
Shelby, this is better than good. You enter it in the art show and you'll see just how good you are.

                    SHELBY
                    (Grins)
Thank you.

MRS. SHAW nods. SHELBY walks away.

                                        CUT TO:

EXT.---YOUNG'S STREET---DAY.

SHELBY and PERCY walk home from school. SHELBY is excited about the art show.

                    PERCY
Good for you, Shelby Sue!

                    SHELBY
Mrs. Shaw even thinks I can win a prize for it!

PERCY

You are good, Shelby. Don't ever let
anyone tell you otherwise.

SHELBY

The show is in two weeks. Maybe Aunt
Cilla will come and see it, too.

PERCY
(Knows Better)

Maybe.

They walk up the driveway.

CUT TO:

INT.---YOUNG HOUSE---DAY.

SHELBY and PERCY walk into the house.
SHELBY glances at the scrapbook on the
coffee table. It is exactly as she left it. She
and PERCY walk into the kitchen, plop their
book bags onto the kitchen table, then
SHELBY goes to the refrigerator for a
snack. PERCY, however, heads for the
bedroom.

SHELBY

Percy, don't you want a popsicle?

PERCY

In a minute, Shel. I got to talk with Mama
first.

71

SHELBY gets herself a popsicle.

CUT TO:

INT.---BERNICE'S BEDROOM---DAY.

PERCY has just told BERNICE the truth of
where she was the night before.

BERNICE
So, you're telling me that you were at the
lighthouse with Rodney, and not at the
Dairy Queen with Twyla?

PERCY
Yes, ma'am.

BERNICE
I'm very disappointed in you, Percy.

PERCY
I know, Mama, I'm sorry.

BERNICE
You're going to be grounded for two weeks
for lying to me, and another two for
sneaking out with a boy!

PERCY
Yes, ma'am. Can I go do my homework
now?

                    BERNICE
Yeah.

PERCY goes to leave, but BERNICE stops
her.

                    BERNICE
Why you telling me this, Percy? Someone
catch you or something?

                    PERCY
No. It just wasn't right, Mama. If I start
doing things that ain't right now, I'm going
to be doing not right things for the rest of
my life.

BERNICE nods.

PERCY goes to leave, but then she turns
around and hugs BERNICE.

                    PERCY
I love you, Mama, and I know you love me.

                    BERNICE
Well, I do. Very much so.

BERNICE is a little perplexed, but
reciprocates the embrace.

                                    CUT TO:

INT.---KITCHEN---DAY.

SHELBY helps DAIVA unload grocery
bags. PERCY bounds into the room, with
the weight of her lie off her shoulders.

                    PERCY
Hey, G-ma!

PERCY joins right in, unloading the bags.

                    PERCY
Shelby, did you tell Grandma about the art
show?

                    SHELBY
No.
                    DAIVA
                    (Brusque)
What art show?

                    PERCY
Miss Shelby's got a drawing good enough to
be entered into the Sapelo Community Art
Show next month! Mrs. Shaw thinks Shelby
could win a prize! We could have a budding
artiste in our house!

                    DAIVA
Yeah, well, drawing pictures never put food
on anyone's table or clothes on anyone's
back. Only fools chase dreams all over the
world and come back with nothing to show.

While SHELBY and PERCY unload the

bags, DAIVA folds up the empty paper
bags.

SHELBY

It's just a contest. I never said I was going
to be Picasso.

DAIVA

Don't get smart with me, young lady. I'm
just telling you how life really is.

PERCY

Well, I'm proud of you, Miss Shelby, and so
is Mama.

DAIVA

I never said I wasn't proud, Percy. I don't
want you girls growing up with a false sense
of how things really are. Dreaming is just
an excuse for irresponsibility!

While DAIVA has her back turned, PERCY
rolls her eyes and shakes her head.
SHELBY smiles. PERCY pats her on the
back.

SHELBY

Where's Aunt Cilla?

DAIVA

Gone.

                         SHELBY
                      (Disappointed)
Oh.

                          DAIVA
She's never coming back here, either,
Shelby, so you might as well just forget
about her. I don't want to hear her name
spoken in this house again. Funny her name
should come up while we are talking about
irresponsibility.

DAIVA folds up the last paper bag, then
leaves SHELBY and PERCY alone.
SHELBY is disappointed, but she keeps
going about her business and puts the food
in the cupboard.

                                          CUT TO:

INT.---SHELBY'S ROOM---NIGHT.

SHELBY lies on the floor and draws a
picture of her and Cilla watching the storm
together.

                                       DISSOLVE TO:

INT.---SAPELO CITY HALL---DAY.

It is the day of the art show. MRS. SHAW
stands beside SHELBY as she is presented
with the first place ribbon for her drawing.

SHELBY smiles, shyly, as she accepts the ribbon. In the audience, PERCY and BERNICE clap and cheer her on.

DISSOLVE TO:

MONTAGE SEQUNECE: Scrapbook #5

SHELBY opens up a brand new scrapbook. The dedication on the first page reads as follows: "You will, because you can. Dream big, Shelby. Love, Percy." SHELBY smiles. She places the drawing and the ribbon into the book.

MRS. SHAW works with SHELBY in art class.

SHELBY and PERCY play catch with a softball in the front yard.

SHELBY wins a first place ribbon, for a self-portrait that she has drawn, in the Sapelo Junior High art show.

SHELBY sits on the porch swing and watches as PERCY pulls into the driveway, honking the horn. HANSON sits in the passenger seat. PERCY parks the car, then gets out and runs to the porch to show SHELBY her drivers license.

SHELBY draws a picture of a southern

plantation, complete with trees dripping with Spanish moss.

SHELBY talks with MRS. SHAW about the drawing.

SHELBY pages through her scrapbook.

END MONTAGE:

CUT TO:

EXT.---YOUNG HOUSE---DAY.

SUPERIMPOSE: SEPTEMBER, 1988.

SHELBY sits on the porch swing. She doesn't have her sketch pad with her. She just sits, sullen.

BERNICE (O.S.)
Percy! You are going to be late if you don't hurry up!!

SHELBY looks towards the house.

PERCY (O.S.)
Mama, I won't be late!

SHELBY smiles, then looks back out at the yard. PERCY bounds out of the front door, onto the porch.

78

PERCY

Man, o'live, they all need to just chill out.
Shelby Sue, what are you doing sitting out
here all by yourself?

SHELBY

Nothing.

PERCY senses that there is something
wrong.

PERCY

Nothing. You're always doing nothing.

PERCY sits beside her on the swing.

SHELBY

It's going to be quiet without you around.

PERCY

Just think of all the drawing you'll have
time to do while I'm at school! And, when I
come home, you better have lots to show
me.

SHELBY just smiles.

PERCY

What am I going to do without you, Miss
Shelby?

SHELBY

What am I going to do without you?

PERCY smiles, then grabs SHELBY in a strong embrace.

SHELBY squeezes PERCY tight as she begins to cry.

PERCY
You're going to be just fine, Shelby Sue. You're a tough cookie! You'll be just fine.

CUT TO:

SHELBY, DAIVA, and HANSON stand on the porch and wave goodbye, as BERNICE and PERCY pull out of the driveway. PERCY waves goodbye. SHELBY walks down to the end of the driveway and watches until the car is no longer visible. She turns back to the house and slowly walks towards it.

CUT TO:

INT.---SAPELO HIGH SCHOOL---DAY.

SHELBY walks through the crowded hall with all the other FRESHMEN. SHELBY finally makes her way to her locker. She tries to open it, but it is stuck. She struggles with it, until JUSTIN DOUGLAS, a fellow freshman, walks up and helps her open it.

                    JUSTIN
There you go.

                    SHELBY
Thank you.

                    JUSTIN
I'm Justin Douglas.

                    SHELBY
Shelby Young.

                    JUSTIN
Nice to meet you, Shelby. My locker's right
next to yours, so if you need help again, just
holler!

SHELBY nods. JUSTIN walks away.
SHELBY watches him as he walks away.
She smiles.

                    DISSOLVE TO:

MONTAGE SEQUENCE: Justin

SHELBY writes a letter to Percy.

                    SHELBY (V.O.)
Dear Percy, how, ya doing? How is
college? I hope you are doing well. So far,
high school is ok. I made friends with a girl
who just moved here. She's from
Cleveland. Her name is Amanda. I've also

been hanging out with Justin. He's not my
boyfriend or anything, he's just a good
friend. The three of us just pretty much hang
out together. How about you? Making a lot
of friends? I bet you are---how could you
not? How are your classes? I'm doing
good. I got an A on my first term paper and
I got an A on my first art project. I miss you
a lot, Perc. I can't wait 'til you come home!
I'll write again soon. Love, Shelby. Oh, I
drew a picture of Justin, so you could see
what he looks like! Yeah, I think he's kind
of cute!

SHELBY and JUSTIN walk down the hall
together.

SHELBY and JUSTIN watch a high school
football game together.

SHELBY eats lunch with JUSTIN and
AMANADA CHAPIN in the school
cafeteria.

SHELBY drawing a portrait of JUSTIN.

CUT TO:

EXT.---SAPELO HIGH FOOTBALL
FIELD---NIGHT.

SUPERIMPOSE: OCTOBER, 1989.

It is Friday night and the Sapelo High Sabers are finishing up a game with St. Simon's Lights. The teams line up; the Sabers on offense, the Lights on defense. The SABERS' QUARTERBACK receives the snap, then immediately takes a knee and the game is over. He raises the ball up in victory, then the TEAMS run off the field.

CUT TO:

INT.---SAPELO HIGH FOOTBALL STADIUM---NIGHT.

SHELBY, JUSTIN and AMANDA stand and cheer for the Sabers. They make their way out of the bleachers.

AMANDA
I'll see you guys at school Monday. I haven't even started my term paper yet, so I'll be working on that all weekend.

SHELBY
Mine's already done.

AMANDA
Shelby! I'll see you guys.

JUSTIN
Bye, Amanda.

                    SHELBY
Bye.

AMANDA walks away.

                    JUSTIN
What do you feel like doing, Shelby?

                    SHELBY
I don't know. How about you?

                    JUSTIN
You ever been out to the lighthouse?

                    SHELBY
Sure. Me and my cousin Percy go fishing
there all the time.

                    JUSTIN
Yeah, but you've never been to the
lighthouse with me!

                    SHELBY
No, I haven't.

                    JUSTIN
Well, let's go then!

                                        CUT TO:

EXT.---SAPELO LIGHTHOUSE---NIGHT.

To establish. The lighthouse beacon flashes

a steady white flash every fifteen seconds.

CUT TO:

INT.---SAPELO LIGHTHOUSE---NIGHT.

JUSTIN leads the way inside the old
lighthouse tower.

JUSTIN

Wow. Look at this, Shelby. Isn't this
incredible?

SHELBY

I've sketched this lighthouse a dozen times,
but I've never seen the inside. It's pretty
cool.

JUSTIN

Pretty cool? Shelby, do you understand the
history here? This lighthouse is over a
hundred and fifty years old! It was built in
1820. The old light keepers had to climb
these stairs dozens of times a night to keep
the lamp lit. This old tower has seen
hundreds of shipwrecks and acts of heroism.
During the Civil War, the Confederates took
out the lantern before the Union soldiers
captured it. And then, there was a hurricane
in 1898 that caused all this damage. It was
finally deactivated in 1905. Only recently
have they started fixing it up.

SHELBY walks to the window and peers out of it.

                    SHELBY

How do you know so much about the lighthouse, Justin?

                    JUSTIN

It's just a hobby. I love history and this old lighthouse is full of it. (pause) You would have been a good light keeper, Shelby.

                    SHELBY

You think so?

                    JUSTIN

I know so. You're strong, independent. Don't mind being alone. Yeah, you would have been a good one.

                    SHELBY

Yeah. I would have had a lot of time to draw too.

                    JUSTIN

Come on. Let's climb to the top.

JUSTIN leads the way as they climb the winding staircase.

                                        CUT TO:

INT.---SAPELO LIGHTHOUSE

LANTERN ROOM---NIGHT.
SHELBY and JUSTIN step out onto the
parapet surrounding the lantern room. The
view is breathtaking, with only the
moonlight glowing on the water.

SHELBY

Wow.

JUSTIN

Amazing view, huh?

SHELBY

It is.

They both lean on the railing and stare out at
the marsh below, while waiting for the
beacon to shine again.

SHELBY

Must have been a lot of work tending one of
these things.

JUSTIN

Oh, it was. The keeper had to stay up all
night and make sure the lamp stayed lit.
During the day, they had to polish the lens,
trim the wicks. Make sure everything was
ready for the night watch.

SHELBY

Kind of takes some of the romance out of it.

JUSTIN

Not for me, it doesn't.

JUSTIN and SHELBY just look at each
other. After a moment, JUSTIN awkwardly
kisses SHELBY for the first time.

SHELBY
(Smiles)
That was my first kiss.

JUSTIN

Mine too. I don't kiss just anybody, you
know!

SHELBY

Neither do I.

They laugh and kiss again.

DISSOLVE TO:

EXT.---SAPELO LIGHTHOUSE
LANTERN ROOM---NIGHT.

SHELBY sits beside JUSTIN at the top of
the lighthouse. They hold hands as they
lean against the lantern room. They just sit
and talk.

JUSTIN
It sure is a beautiful night, Shelby.

SHELBY

It is.

JUSTIN

I'd like to tell you that I love you, but I
know you won't believe me.

SHELBY

You're right. You don't know me well
enough to love me.

JUSTIN

Shelby, I've known you for over a year now.
But I don't think I'll ever know you well
enough for you to believe that I love you.
Sometimes I think you'd be just as content
to sit up here with a sketch pad and pencil,
as you would be to sit here with me.

SHELBY shrugs.

JUSTIN

You know, I'm right. You're just that kind
of person, Shelby; independent; can take
care of yourself; most of the time content
just to be on your own. You don't really
seem to need anybody. That's what scares
me about you, Shel.

SHELBY
(Rare Candor)

It scares me too, Justin, but that's just how I
am.

89

JUSTIN nods.

                    SHELBY
But, that doesn't mean I'll always be that
way. Maybe there is someone who can
change that. Maybe that's you.

JUSTIN smiles.

                    JUSTIN
Well, all right then!

                    SHELBY
Enough of this serious stuff. Let's just
enjoy the night, look at the stars and the
water.

                    JUSTIN
Whatever you want, Miss Shelby. Whatever
you want.

They lean back and look at the stars.

JUSTIN points out a constellation which
SHELBY admires.

                                        CUT TO:

INT.---DOUGLAS HOUSE---NIGHT.
The DOUGLAS FAMILY is putting up the
Christmas tree. SHELBY and JUSTIN
place the ornaments, while MR. DOUGLAS
strings popcorn, with Justin's sister,

LYNETTE.

MRS. DOUGLAS enters the room carrying
a tray of eggnog.

MRS. DOUGLAS
Shelby, Justin, I got some eggnog here.

SHELBY
Thank you, Mrs. Douglas.

MRS. DOUGLAS
You're welcome, dear.

SHELBY hangs her ornament, then walks
over to the tray and picks up a glass of
eggnog. JUSTIN joins her.

MRS. DOUGLAS
The tree looks great you guys.

SHELBY
Thank you.

MRS. DOUGLAS
Are you going to stay for supper, Shelby?

SHELBY
I'd love to Mrs. Douglas, but my cousin
Percy's coming home today!

                    MRS. DOUGLAS
Oh, that's right. Justin told me that. I hope
we'll get to see you for the holiday.

                      SHELBY
Justin invited me for Christmas Eve dinner.

                    MRS. DOUGLAS
Oh, good!

                      SHELBY
I'm going to get going. Percy should be
home soon, I want to be there waiting for
her.

JUSTIN walks SHELBY to the door.

                      SHELBY
Goodnight, Mr. & Mrs. Douglas. Lynette.

                   DOUGLAS FAMILY
Bye, Shelby.

SHELBY and JUSTIN walk outside.

                      JUSTIN
Goodnight, Shelby.

                      SHELBY
Goodnight.

She kisses JUSTIN goodbye, then hurries
down the driveway as JUSTIN watches her.

EXT.---YOUNG HOUSE---NIGHT.
SHELBY sits on the swing, anxiously
awaiting Percy's arrival. HANSON sits on
the porch, while DAIVA stands inside and
looks out the screen door. BERNICE paces
the porch and checks her watch.

                    BERNICE
She should have been here a half hour ago.

                    HANSON
She should have flown. I told her I would
buy her a ticket.

                    BERNICE
Oh no, Daddy. You know Percy, she's so
damn stubborn. She had to drive from New
York.

                    HANSON
Gee, I wonder where she gets that from?

                    BERNICE
Not me.

                    SHELBY
Probably Aunt Cilla.

HANSON and BERNICE both look at her,
then they go back to their "worrying"
positions.

Finally, PERCY pulls into the driveway.

SHELBY stands up and DAIVA comes outside.

PERCY quickly shuts off the car, and bounds out of the car. One and a half years of college have matured Percy, but have not changed her infectious nature.

> PERCY

Hey! I'm home!!

PERCY hurries up the stairs and hugs BERNICE.

> PERCY

Mama!

> BERNICE

What took you so long?

> PERCY

Oh, Mama, I'm only a half hour late!

She hugs HANSON.

> PERCY

Granddaddy!

> HANSON

Welcome home, Perc.

PERCY looks at DAIVA.

                    PERCY
Hey, G-ma!

                    DAIVA
Glad you're home safe, Percy.

PERCY saves the best for last.

                    PERCY
Shelby Sue! Come here, kiddo!

She grabs SHELBY in a giant bear-hug and
squeezes her tight.

                    PERCY
I have missed you soo much, Shelby!

                    SHELBY
I've missed you more, Perc!

PERCY laughs.

                                        CUT TO:

INT.---PERCY'S ROOM---NIGHT.

SHELBY helps PERCY unpack her stuff.

                    SHELBY
So, how is New York, Perc?

95

PERCY

Oh my God, Shelby, it is amazing! I love everything about it, the city, the people, my classes---everything. There is a whole other world outside of Sapelo, Shelby. I can see now why Aunt Cilla wanted to leave this place---but I don't understand how she could leave her family. I miss you and Mama, so much. I wish you guys were with me.

SHELBY

If Grandma and Grandpa would ever let me, I'd come visit, but you know Grandma. Everything's always too much money or too much trouble. I wish I could get out of here.

PERCY

Your time will come, Shelby. You keep up with your studies and your artwork, get yourself a scholarship. But for now, enjoy the moment. And Justin.

SHELBY smiles.

PERCY

Ahh, I knew it! Little Shelby Sue is growing up. That there is the smile of a woman in love!

SHELBY

Oh come on, Perc. I'm hardly a woman, and I'm hardly in love.

PERCY

No, maybe not yet, but I am, Shelby. And
let me tell you, that is wonderful too!

SHELBY

What's his name?

PERCY

His name is David and he is just the most
wonderful guy. I never met anyone else like
him, Shel. He brings out the best in me like
no one ever has. That's what love is. Makes
you a better person.

SHELBY

I think Justin makes me a better person.

PERCY

So, do you love him?

SHELBY

I don't know. Maybe I do.

PERCY

Well, you got time to figure that out, Shelby.

PERCY stops suddenly.

PERCY

Uh-oh. You two haven't…you know…

SHELBY

No.

PERCY

Ok, that's good. That there is something
you don't give out to just anyone, Shelby
Sue. That's something precious you want to
hold onto and save only for someone who
you know you love and you know loves you.

SHELBY

Like David?

PERCY

Yes, like David! But I waited a long time,
until the time was right by my choosing. I
worry about you sometimes, Shelby,
because I ain't around to guide you like I
should be. God knows G-ma isn't going to
steer you right.

SHELBY

No one wants me to make the same mistake
my mother made.

PERCY

Oh, Shelby, you are no mistake. You are a
gift to all of us. Someday, they'll all realize
that. Including your mama.

SHELBY

Wherever she is.

PERCY

All right, enough of this! Let's get that tree

up and decorated before G-ma starts having
a cow!

PERCY heads to the door, with SHELBY
right behind.

                    SHELBY
I've really missed you, Perc.

                    PERCY
I've missed you more, kiddo!

                                        CUT TO:

MONTAGE SEQUENCE: Christmas Time

SHELBY eats Christmas Eve dinner with
the DOUGLAS FAMILY.

Christmas morning, the YOUNG FAMILY
opens up gifts. SHELBY opens up a
"NYU" sweatshirt from PERCY.

The YOUNGS eat dinner. PERCY regales
them with tales from college.

JUSTIN gives SHELBY a gift. She opens it.
It is a gold necklace with a small lighthouse
charm. She kisses him.

JUSTIN opens his gift, which is a beautiful
portrait that Shelby drew of the two of them
sitting at the lighthouse. He is excited by

the picture. He kisses her.

SHELBY lies on her floor and draws a
picture of dinner at the Douglas house.
She places the drawing into yet another full
scrapbook. She sticks the completed
scrapbook on a shelf with the nine other
completed books.

CUT TO:

EXT.---YOUNG HOUSE----DAY.

HANSON helps PERCY load up the car.
HANSON closes the trunk, then walks back
up to the porch. PERCY walks to the porch
too.

PERCY
Thanks, Granddaddy.

HANSON
Have a safe trip, Percy.

He hugs her, then goes and sits on the swing
with DAIVA. SHELBY and BERNICE
stand off to the side.

PERCY
Bye, G-ma.

SHELBY
Bye, Perc.

They hug, a long goodbye embrace.

                    PERCY
Mama.

PERCY and BERNICE hug. BERNICE is
tearful.

                    BERNICE
I hate it every time you leave, Miss Percy.

                    PERCY
I'll be home again, real soon, Mama. Don't
you worry.

                    BERNICE
Get going. I don't want you driving too
long in the dark.

                    PERCY
Oh, I'll be fine, Mama. Life's too short to
worry all the time! Bye, y'all!

With that, PERCY gets into the car.
SHELBY runs up to the window. PERCY
unrolls the window.

                    SHELBY
I do love him, Perc!

PERCY
(Smiles)
I told you, Miss Shelby! You can't fool me.
I love you, kiddo!

SHELBY
I love you, too!

PERCY turns on the car and backs out of the
drive way. She honks the horn, waves out
the window, then disappears on the horizon.

CUT TO:

INT.---YOUNG HOUSE---NIGHT.

To establish. DAIVA and HANSON sleep.
BERNICE sleeps. SHELBY is sound
asleep. The PHONE rings. It rings
incessantly, until BERNICE finally answers
it. SHELBY remains asleep.

BERNICE (O.S.)
Hello. (pause) This is her. (pause) No. No!
(Wails)
Noooo!

DISSOLVE TO:

INT.---YOUNG HOUSE---NIGHT

BERNICE sits on the couch and sobs,
continually and uncontrollably. HANSON

walks around the room, rubbing his
forehead.

In the kitchen DAIVA prepares a cup of
coffee for Bernice. She carries it into the
living room, places it on the coffee table,
then sits beside her daughter, as BERNICE
continues to sob.

                                    CUT TO:

EXT.---YOUNG HOUSE---NIGHT.

SHELBY sits alone on the swing, slowly
rocking back and forth. Silent tears roll
down her face.

                              DISSOLVE TO:

EXT.---YOUNG HOUSE---DAY.

SHELBY sits on the swing. She has been
there all night. JUSTIN now sits beside her.
SHELBY delivers the news of Percy's
death, to Justin.

                    SHELBY
She was in a car accident. She was about
two hours out of New York when the storm
hit. (laughs) What's a little snow to Percy?
It wasn't going to stop her. (pause) She hit a
patch of ice and smashed right into the
guard rail. The police said she died

                       103

instantly---wasn't wearing her seat belt.
Nothing ever held Percy back, you think she
was going to wear a damn seatbelt?

She begins to tear up, but fights it. JUSTIN
holds SHELBY as she cries for her beloved
cousin.

CUT TO:

EXT.---SAPELO CEMETARY---DAY.

About 50 mourners are gathered at the
funeral of PERCY ELIZABETH ELLISON.
SHELBY, BERNICE, DAIVA, and
HANSON stand closest to the casket.
DAVID MADSON, Percy's boyfriend,
stands beside SHELBY. JUSTIN stands
towards the back of the CROWD with his
parents, MR. & MRS. DOUGLAS. Percy's
casket is covered with bright yellow and red
roses, that reflect Percy's bright personality.
BERNICE cries; DAIVA is stoic; HANSON
bows his head to hide his tears. SHELBY
just stares at Percy's casket, fighting hard to
control her tears.

FR. MATT RHODES sprinkles the casket
with holy water.

SHELBY continues to stare at the casket.

FR. RHODES (O.S.)
…May the angels lead you to paradise.
Heavenly Father, please welcome our
daughter Percy into your loving kingdom
where she will live with you forever and be
a guardian to those she has left behind.
Father, mercifully look upon your children
and comfort them in their time of grief.

FR. RHODES pauses and looks around at
the MOURNERS.

FR. RHODES
May God bless you all, in the name of the
father and of the son, and of the holy spirit,
amen.

ALL make the sign of the cross, except for
SHELBY. BERNICE walks up to the casket
and places a small bouquet of daisies on the
casket. She gently touches the casket, then
sobs. HANSON helps her along. DAIVA
places a rose on the casket. SHELBY places
a rose onto the casket, then quickly walks
away. DAVID kisses a rose, then places it
on the casket.

JUSTIN watches as SHELBY separates
herself from the MOURNERS. She stands
alone, some distance from the funeral tent.
JUSTIN takes his place in line.

CUT TO:

EXT.---CEMETARY---DAY.

SHELBY stands and watches the funeral from a distance. Her eyes are red and tears slowly stream down her face.

JUSTIN walks up to her.

                    JUSTIN
How ya doing?

SHELBY quickly wipes her eyes.

                    SHELBY
I'm fine.

He reaches for her arm, but she brusquely walks away.

                    JUSTIN
You sure?

                    SHELBY
Yeah.

                    JUSTIN
                    (Hurt)
Shelby. Whatever you want me to do for you, tell me and I will do it.

                    SHELBY
Percy's dead, Justin. There isn't anything you can do to make that better. I just want

to be alone for awhile.

JUSTIN
(Hurt)
Ok.

JUSTIN takes another look at SHELBY,
who doesn't look back at him, then he
slowly walks away.

DISSOLVE TO:

EXT.---SAPELO LIGHTHOUSE---DAY.

SHELBY sits across from the lighthouse, at
the pond where she and Percy used to fish.
She sketches the lighthouse, but then she
stops and reflects.

CUT TO:

FLASHBACK: SHELBY and PERCY sit in
their row boat, fishing. PERCY drops some
chew into SHELBY'S open mouth.

CUT TO:

FLASHBACK: SHELBY catches a fish, but
she struggles to reel it in. PERCY stands up
in the boat and tries to help SHELBY, but
she rocks the boat. She falls down into the
boat and SHELBY starts laughing so hard
that she lets go of her rod, which the fish

pulls into the water. Both girls burst into
uncontrollable laughter.

CUT TO:

SHELBY sits and stares vacantly. Tears roll
down her face. Tears have fallen on her
lighthouse sketch, smudging the drawing.

CUT TO:

INT.---YOUNG HOUSE---NIGHT.

HANSON sits and watches TV, while
DAIVA sits beside him and crochets.

SHELBY enters the front door. She walks
into the living room, then heads for the
hallway, but DAIVA stops her.

DAIVA
It's after nine on a school night. Where
have you been?

SHELBY
Out.

DAIVA
That's not an answer, young lady.

SHELBY
It's the best I've got.

SHELBY walks away.

DAIVA
(Mad)
Shelby Suzanne Young, don't---

HANSON
Dee, let her alone.

DAIVA is still mad, but she listens to
HANSON.

CUT TO:

INT.---PERCY'S ROOM---NIGHT.

BERNICE sits on Percy's bed and folds her
clothes. SHELBY walks into the room.

SHELBY
What are you doing?

BERNICE
Sorting Percy's things.

SHELBY
Can I help?

BERNICE
Sure.

SHELBY sits beside BERNICE and starts
folding Percy's clothes. BERNICE picks up

one of Percy's old baseball jerseys. She
looks at it.

                    BERNICE
Percy was such a tom boy, but look at what
a lovely young lady she turned out to be,
huh?

SHELBY just nods.

                    BERNICE
Parents aren't supposed to bury their
children, Shelby. It's just not right. I
suppose if I was more like you're Mama,
this whole thing might be easier---would be
easier. She essentially buried you the day
you were born. She buried you and never
looked back. How could she do that to you,
Shelby? I never really thought much about
it, but now…Percy was my life. I love her
so much and now I don't have her. It's just
not fair…

                    SHELBY
Am I like her? My mother?

                    BERNICE
You look like her more so than your dad---

                    SHELBY
That's not what I meant. Am I like her, like
she is or was?

                    BERNICE
Your Mama never needed anyone.

SHELBY nods.

                    SHELBY
Neither do I.

BERNICE just looks at her, smirks and
shakes her head. SHELBY continues to fold
clothes.

                                        CUT TO:

INT.---SAPELO HIGH ART ROOM---
DAY.

SHELBY'S art class has just ended.

SHELBY walks up to the teacher, MRS.
DONOHUE.

                    MRS. DONOHUE
Yes, Shelby.

                    SHELBY
Do you mind if I stay after to work on my
portrait?

                    MRS. DONOHUE
No, not at all. I'll be here 'til about 4:30. I
don't mind if you stay.

                    SHELBY
Thanks.

                                        CUT TO:

INT.---SAPELO HIGH ART ROOM---
DAY.

SHELBY sits at her easel and works on a
portrait of Percy.

JUSTIN, carrying his books under his arm,
walks into the room.

                    JUSTIN
Hi, Shelby.

SHELBY looks at him, then goes back to
her drawing.
                    SHELBY
Hi, Justin.

                    JUSTIN
Missed you at lunch today.

                    SHELBY
I had a test to make up.

                    JUSTIN
Oh.

He sits across from her, but she remains
focused.

JUSTIN

How was your first day back?

SHELBY

Fine.

JUSTIN nods. They continue on in
awkward silence for a moment before
JUSTIN speaks.

JUSTIN

You're work is beautiful, as always.

SHELBY

Justin---

JUSTIN

Shelby, listen. I've given you space, but I
can see you're hurting and I just want to be
with you. You need a friend right now.

SHELBY

No, I just need to be alone.

JUSTIN

That's bull, Shelby! You need me.

SHELBY finally puts her pencil down and
looks at JUSTIN.

SHELBY

Justin…when you held me the day after
Percy died, it felt so good. I never felt so

113

safe, as I did that morning with you. I felt like somehow you could make anything right. But I know better, Justin. Someday, you'll leave too. But, I'm not going to let you, because I'm going to leave first this time. Anyone I've ever cared about or loved, or who should have loved me, is gone. My mother left me in the hospital, the day I was born. When I was eight, my best friend moved away…my Aunt Cilla comes and goes…and now Percy, the only person who's ever really given a damn about me, is dead! And I know, somehow, someday, you're going to leave too, so this is just how it's got to be, Justin. No matter how much it hurts now, it will save me a lot more hurt in the future.

JUSTIN

Shelby, this is crazy! You don't know what you are saying! You're just upset about Percy---

SHELBY

This has nothing to do with Percy, it has everything to do with me. I don't need anyone. Besides, what good are people if they're just going to leave?

JUSTIN

Shelby…

                    SHELBY

Remember that night at the lighthouse, when
you said I could be just as happy with a
pencil and a sketch pad? You were right.

                    JUSTIN

Shelby, those are just pictures, you can't be
happy with pictures.

                    SHELBY

Pictures last, Justin. People don't.

SHELBY gathers her pad and pencils.

                    SHELBY

Goodbye, Justin.

She walks out the door, down the hall and
never looks back.

                  JUSTIN (O.S.)

Shelby, don't do this! You know you need
me, you're just quitting because you're sad
and confused! Shelby, please! Let me help
you! Shelby!

                              DISSOLVE TO:

MONTAGE SEQUENCE: The Wall

SHELBY walks into the house, carrying her
portrait under her arm and her book bag
over her shoulder. HANSON watches TV.

DAIVA prepares dinner. BERNICE sits at the kitchen table, folding napkins. She walks through the living room into her bedroom without speaking a word. She sets the portrait down, then her book bag. She lies on the floor and reflects.

DISSOLVE TO:

SHELBY walks through the crowded hall at school. She passes by her locker, where JUSTIN and DENISE SMITH stand and talk. She looks at them. JUSTIN looks back at her briefly, then he turns back to DENISE. SHELBY just walks on .

SHELBY works on her portrait of Percy.

SHELBY'S portrait of Percy, wins first prize in the juried high school art show. She walks up onto the stage to accept her award. No one is there to watch.

SHELBY sitting by the lighthouse, drawing a self-portrait. The self-portrait is cold, reflecting Shelby's hardened spirit. Yet, it reveals an aura of strength.

END MONTAGE:

CUT TO:

EXT.---YOUNG HOUSE---DAY.

SUPERIMPOSE: 1992

SHELBY steps off of the bus. She gets the mail out of the mail box and leafs through it as she walks up the driveway. She stops and looks at one letter in particular. She opens it, reads it and smiles. She continues her walk up the drive.

                                        CUT TO:

INT.---YOUNG HOUSE---DAY.

SHELBY sets the table, while DAIVA prepares dinner.

                    DAIVA
I don't think you should go.

                    SHELBY
That doesn't surprise me.

                    DAIVA
Why would you say that?

                    SHELBY
You've never supported me in anything I've ever done or wanted to do, so why should you now?

                    DAIVA
Shelby, I don't support non-sense. What kind of career are you going to have

drawing pictures?

SHELBY

There are a lot of things I can do and what difference does it make anyway? It's a full scholarship to one of the best art schools in the country.

DAIVA

I've watched my other daughters---your mother---walk out of here chasing nonsense dreams and I know where it got them---nowhere!

SHELBY

I'm not your real daughter, isn't that what you've always been so quick to tell other people? You think you'd be happy, 'cause you can finally be rid of me.

DAIVA

Shelby, don't be ridiculous.

SHELBY

No, it's no secret how you've felt about having to raise me. Why deny it? And you know what, it doesn't even matter what you say, because I'm going.

SHELBY sets the last place setting, then walks away. DAIVA sighs then continues to cook.

EXT.---YOUNG PORCH---NIGHT.

SHELBY sits on the porch and thinks.

HANSON walks out and sits beside her.

                    HANSON
What ya doing?

                    SHELBY
Sittin'.

There is a moment of silence.

                    HANSON
A full scholarship, huh?

                    SHELBY
Four years at the New York Institute of Art.

                    HANSON
That's pretty good. When are you leaving?

                    SHELBY
July. I want to get there and get a job before
school starts. I've got my savings to start
out with.

HANSON nods. He reaches into his pocket
and pulls out an envelope of money.

HANSON

I want you to have this. Make things a little easier for you.

SHELBY takes it and looks inside. There is a thousand dollars in it.

SHELBY

You don't have to do this.

HANSON

I want to. (pause) When Bernice married Bob, she moved to Jacksonville right after the wedding. She didn't come back until he died in 'Nam. Your mother left...(Shakes his head) and Cilla left and only came back when she had no where else to go. But your leaving is different. Even Percy leaving wasn't the same. You see, they all came back. You're not coming back, Shelby, and that's ok.

SHELBY just nods.

HANSON'S eyes tear up, but he does not cry.

CUT TO:

EXT.---YOUNG HOUSE---DAY.

BERNICE and HANSON watch as SHELBY puts her last suit case in her trunk.

She closes the trunk. BERNICE gives her a hug, then HANSON nods and waves. DAIVA stands behind the screen door and watches.

SHELBY gets into the car and drives away.

DAIVA walks away from the screen door.

CUT TO:

INT.---SHELBY'S ROOM---DAY.

DAIVA stands in the doorway and looks around the empty room. The room is stripped of anything that is a reminder of Shelby. Even the bed is stripped of bedding, just a bare mattress and a pillow. DAIVA walks over to the bed, softly touches the pillow, then walks to the window. She looks out the window and adjusts the café curtain that hangs in the window.

CUT TO:

EXT.---NEW YORK CITY---DAY.

Series of establishing shots.

CUT TO:

INT.---NY INSTITUTE OF ART LIBRARY---DAY.

SHELBY looks through the shelves for a
particular book. Sitting at a table not too far
off, is PAUL RYCE. He reads a book, but
every so often, he looks up at SHELBY.
She is oblivious to his attention. SHELBY
moves down another aisle. Finally, PAUL
gets up and walks over to her.

PAUL

Excuse me. This is going to sound like the
worst come on, but I promise you it's not.
I've seen you around campus all semester
and you look so familiar to me, but I can't
place you.

SHELBY

You're right. That was the worst come on.

PAUL

No, I'm serious.

SHELBY

So am I! That was pathetic.

PAUL

I know you from somewhere…what's your
name?

SHELBY

Shelby Young.

PAUL smiles.

PAUL

Shelby Young. From Sapelo Island?

SHELBY

Yeah.

PAUL

I'm Paul Ryce! You of course used to know
me as Palmer Ryce!

SHELBY breaks into a wide smile.

SHELBY

Palmer Ryce! You're Palmer Ryce?

He smiles and nods.

CUT TO:

EXT.---NYIA CAMPUS---DAY.

The campus is bathed in fallen Autumn
leaves, yet the sun shines on this crisp
afternoon. SHELBY and PAUL walk and
talk.

SHELBY

I can't believe you remembered me!

PAUL

Of course I remember you. You were my
best friend in Sapelo. We used to play tic-

tac-toe at recess and if I remember correctly
you beat me pretty handily most times!

SHELBY laughs at the memory.

SHELBY

I let you win sometimes!

PAUL

I knew it. We used to draw too. Obviously
we're still doing that since we're both here.
But a lot has changed since I left Sapelo. I
can tie my shoes all by myself and I don't
stutter anymore! I go by Paul, now, not
Palmer. Paul is a little more New York.
How about you, what have you been doing
since the third grade?

SHELBY

Ahh, well, I really haven't changed too
much, I guess. Recess was never the same
without you, I kept drawing, and I never left
Sapelo 'til I came here. That's about it.

PAUL

That's it?

SHELBY

That's it. I've pretty much put everything
into my drawings.

PAUL

I'd love to see you're portfolio and show

124

you mine if you'd like.

                    SHELBY
Yeah. I'd like that too.

                    PAUL
                    (Genuine excitement)
So, it's a date, then! Exchange portfolios,
maybe go out for pizza...I can't believe we
met again, Shelby. This is amazing!

SHELBY just smiles.

                                        CUT TO:

INT.---PAUL'S APARTMENT---NIGHT.

SHELBY looks through Paul's portfolio of
paintings and drawings, while PAUL gets
some pop from the kitchen.

                    SHELBY
You got into watercolor, huh?

                    PAUL
Yeah. I really love doing landscapes, but
drawing is still my first love. I have a
summer job doing caricatures at Coney
Island. It's not as detailed of course, but I'm
getting paid to draw. But I don't know if I'll
be there this summer, because I've applied
for a semester in Paris for next fall. Don't
know if I'll get it, but I hope I will.

PAUL enters the room and hands SHELBY
a glass of pop.

SHELBY

These are excellent.

PAUL sits down beside her.

PAUL

Thank you. These ones here of Central Park
are my favorite.

He flips through the portfolio to find the
watercolors of Central Park.

SHELBY

Wow.

PAUL

Have you been drawing in the park yet?

SHELBY

No.

PAUL

Aww, you've got to go, Shelby. I'll have to
take you there before Winter. You can't
wait 'til Spring.

SHELBY

These are all very good, Paul. I'm
impressed.

PAUL

I'm glad. Now, I want to see yours.

CUT TO:

INT.----PAUL'S APARTMENT---DAY.

PAUL sits on the floor and leans against the
couch, as he looks through Shelby's
portfolio. SHELBY sits beside him and
looks over his shoulder.

SHELBY

That's the Sapelo lighthouse. And that's of
the woods across the street from my house.

PAUL turns to a portrait of Percy.

PAUL

Who's that?

SHELBY

My cousin, Percy. Remember her?

PAUL

Yeah, I went with you a few times to watch
her play softball.

SHELBY

She died in a car accident a few years ago.

PAUL

I'm sorry.

SHELBY quickly turns the page.

> SHELBY
>
> This is my Aunt Cilla.

> PAUL
>
> I don't remember her.

> SHELBY
>
> I only saw her a few times. She was never around very long. People I care about usually never are.

> PAUL
>
> Maybe, sometimes, they come back.

SHELBY is reflective for a moment, but then she smiles as she reveals her last drawing.

> SHELBY
>
> Now this one is not part of my portfolio, but I thought you might like it.

It is the drawing that Shelby drew of her and Palmer on the playground in kindergarten.

> PAUL
> (Amused)
> Oh my God! That's awesome, Shelby! I can't believe you still have this!

SHELBY

I've saved all of my drawings. It's just my
way of remembering people and things that
have happened. And, this one here, I drew
after you left.

She turns the page to reveal the drawing of
Shelby sitting beside the empty swing.
PAUL studies the drawing, then looks at
SHELBY and smiles.

SHELBY

What?

PAUL

I'd love to see what you would draw about
tonight.

SHELBY just grins.

CUT TO:

INT.---SHELBY'S APARTMENT---
NIGHT.

SHELBY sits at her easel and draws a
portrait of Paul, sitting, knees drawn up, his
chin resting in his hand, and a sweet smile
on his face.

The time on the alarm clock reads 4:29 a.m.

CUT TO:

EXT.---PAUL'S APARTMENT---NIGHT.

PAUL arrives home to find a wrapped package leaning against his door. He picks it up, then walks into the apartment.

                                        CUT TO:

INT.---PAUL'S APARTMENT---NIGHT.

PAUL unwraps the package and smiles when he sees the drawing. He reads the note that is attached.

                    SHELBY (V.O.)
This is how I want to remember last night. Shelby.

                                DISSOLVE TO:

MONTAGE SEQUENCE: Sometimes, They Come Back

MUSIC: Jewel's "This Way."

SHELBY and PAUL walk through the park, carrying sketch pads and a blanket. PAUL points out a good spot, so they walk to it and lay down their blanket.

                                        CUT TO:

SHELBY sits on the blanket and draws the

bridge and the pond. PAUL sits beside her.
He draws a picture of Shelby drawing.
SHELBY looks over at him and tries to peek
at his drawing, but he pulls the sketchpad
closer to him and shakes his head.

DISSOLVE TO:

PAUL finishes his drawing. He signs it,
then hands it over to SHELBY. She is
pleased with the drawing.

SHELBY walks across campus. PAUL
walks in the opposite direction. He sees
SHELBY. He smiles and waves to her. She
waves and they walk to each other, stop and
talk.

SHELBY and PAUL walk through Central
Park. They stop at the bridge and look at the
water. It begins to snow. SHELBY is
excited---this is her first snowfall. SHELBY
and PAUL kiss for the first time.

SHELBY sits at her desk in her art theory
class. She sketches a small drawing of Paul
in the margin of her notebook.

SHELBY and PAUL sit on the floor of
Paul's apartment, eating pizza and studying.

SHELBY puts a drawing of her and Paul ice
skating into her scrapbook. Scrapbook

number fifteen.

SHELBY and PAUL walk through the
campus as a heavy snow falls. SHELBY
suddenly stops walking, bends down, makes
a snowball and lobs it at PAUL, hitting him
in the back. He laughs, then retaliates.
They engage in a snowball fight, until
PAUL finally grabs SHELBY and dumps
her into the snow. He proceeds to dump
snow on her, but she grabs him and pulls
him into the snow. They both laugh and
scream.

CUT TO:

INT.---SHELBY'S APARTMENT---DAY.

SHELBY, with wet hair, clad in a robe, sits
by the fireplace. She shivers. PAUL,
himself, wrapped in a blanket, walks into the
living room from the kitchen, carrying a cup
of hot tea. He hands the tea to SHELBY,
who quickly sips it.

PAUL
Are you warm yet?

SHELBY nods as she sips the tea. He takes
off the blanket and wraps it around
SHELBY. He sits down beside her.

PAUL

I'm sorry. I forgot, you're not used to New
York winters yet.

SHELBY

I like the snow.

Her teeth chatter as she shivers. She sips the
tea.

PAUL
(Shakes his head)

I'm sorry, Shel.

She nudges him.

SHELBY

Forget it, Paul! I'm fine. I had a good time.
I'd just watch your back if I were you!

PAUL laughs. He looks at SHELBY, who
appears deep in thought.

PAUL

What are you thinking about?

She looks at him.

SHELBY

I can't believe I'm doing this.

PAUL

Doing what?

SHELBY

Falling in love with you.

PAUL

Is that a good can't believe or a bad can't believe?

SHELBY

Both.

PAUL

Well, that's good because I'm falling in love with you too. What's the bad?

SHELBY

It won't last.

PAUL

Sure it will. We'll make it last.

SHELBY

Paul, don't promise me forever, because you can't. Just because you love me doesn't mean you'll always be here, and just because I love you, that pretty much means you won't be. Let's just enjoy us while we last.

PAUL

I'm sorry for whoever or whatever made you feel that way, Shelby...

SHELBY

That's just how it is, you know?

PAUL

No, it doesn't have to be. Not everyone you
care about is going to leave you. I'm not
leaving, Shelby, and I'll do whatever I have
to do to take that fear away from you
because I do love you---you taught me how
to tie my own shoes, how could I not love
you?

SHELBY

I'm serious, Paul.

PAUL

I'm serious too. I'm not going anywhere,
Shelby. I love you.

SHELBY

I want to believe you, Paul.

PAUL

I'll make you believe. Enough of this talk
then, huh? Give me a chance. Give us a
chance.

SHELBY smiles, then kisses PAUL. THEY
share a passionate kiss.

DISSOLVE TO:

INT.---SHELBY'S APARTMENT---
NIGHT.

SHELBY sleeps in PAUL'S arms, in front
of the fireplace.

FADE OUT:

FADE IN EXT.---NYIA CAMPUS---DAY.

To establish. SUPERIMPOSE: SPRING,
1993

CUT TO:

INT.---MAIL ROOM---DAY.

PAUL gets his mail. He shuffles through it,
but he stops at a particular letter. He opens
it, then smiles. He hurries off.

CUT TO:

EXT.---CAMPUS QUAD---DAY.

SHELBY sits on a bench, reading a book
and eating an apple. PAUL hurries over to
her.

PAUL
Shelby! Shelby!

SHELBY
Hey, Paul.

136

He greets her with a kiss and a smile.

                    PAUL
I got it, Shel! I got the scholarship to study
in Paris next semester!

Her smile dims at the news, but for Paul's
sake, the smile doesn't fade.

                                        CUT TO:

INT.---SHELBY'S APARTMENT---DAY.

PAUL sits on the floor and leans against the
couch, as he reads through his Paris
information.

SHELBY stands at the kitchen table and
folds her laundry.

                    PAUL
Listen to this…I get to take classes at the
Louvre and at the Sorbonne! And there are
more practical classes as opposed to theory
classes, so I won't be stuck in a class room
all the time. I'll actually be out, drawing
and painting. This is an incredible program.

                    SHELBY
When do you leave?

                    PAUL
As soon as this semester's finished. I want

to spend the summer there.

SHELBY bristles at the thought of Paul leaving.

PAUL

But, I haven't told you the best part of this yet.

He stands up and walks over to her.

PAUL

I want you to come with me.

SHELBY

It's too late, I can't get into the program.

PAUL

Then just come for the summer or take next semester off! Six months in Paris have got to be worth more than a semester here.

SHELBY nods.

PAUL

Or I will just forget Paris and stay here with you.

SHELBY

(Stunned)

Why would you do that?

PAUL

Because I love you. Regardless of what you

might think, Shelby, there are some things more important than drawing. You are more important to me than anything I could learn or do in Paris.

                    SHELBY
Just when I think you can't amaze me anymore, you do!

                     PAUL
Why does that amaze you? You're more important to me than anything.

                    SHELBY
Well, then I guess I have no choice but to go with you!

PAUL laughs and hugs SHELBY.

                     PAUL
It's going to be great, Shelby! Let's start packing now!

She laughs.

                    SHELBY
Thank you.

He just smiles and kisses her.

                     PAUL
Ok, I'm serious...let's start packing!

                        SHELBY
Ok, ok!

                                        CUT TO:

INT.---SHELBY'S APARTMENT---DAY.

SHELBY is packing her suitcase. Lisa
Loeb's "Stay," plays in the background.

There is a knock on the door. SHELBY
folds one more blouse, tosses it into the
suitcase, then goes to answer the door. She
opens the door to find CILLA standing on
the other side. SHELBY is stunned.
CILLA is contrite as she just stands and
stares at SHELBY. Tears fill her eyes.

                        SHELBY
Aunt Cilla.

After an awkward moment, CILLA grabs
SHELBY in a strong embrace. SHELBY
reluctantly reciprocates.

                                        CUT TO:

INT.---SHELBY'S APARTMENT---DAY.

CILLA sits on the couch and looks around
the apartment. She wipes the tears that are
forming in her eyes, while SHELBY
prepares a cup of tea for her.

SHELBY

I'm sorry I don't have coffee. I don't drink
it.

CILLA

That's ok, Shelby. Tea is fine.

SHELBY enters with the tea and sets it
down on the table in front of CILLA.
SHELBY sits down across from her. She is
leery of Cilla and her intentions.

SHELBY

Why are you here?

CILLA

Because I wanted to see you.

SHELBY

You're just passing through New York, like
you used to pass through Sapelo.

CILLA

No, it's not like that, Shelby. I came here to
see you. You're Grandma and Granddaddy
gave me your address. It's been what, three
or four years since---

SHELBY

Seven.

CILLA nods, then nervously sips her tea.
She sets it down and looks at the floor.

CILLA

I'm dying, Shelby. Ovarian cancer. The
doctors say I can try some experimental
treatments, but even than the chances of
survival are no better. I came here to tell
you something I should have told you years
ago. (pause) Shelby, I'm your mother.

SHELBY closes her eyes briefly and looks
away from CILLA. She gets up and walks
to the window and paces. She nervously
fidgets with a ring that she wears on her
right hand.

CILLA

I know this is probably a big shock for
you...

SHELBY

I always knew that you were my mother.
No one ever told me, I just knew.

CILLA

Why didn't you ever say anything?

SHELBY

I figured you would have told me if you
wanted to.

SHELBY continues to pace by the window.
CILLA can't face her.

SHELBY

I didn't need you, you know? I'm not
saying that to be mean or spiteful. Just
honest. God made me strong. He must have
known I wouldn't have you, so he made me
strong. Made sure I would never need
anyone but me.

CILLA turns and faces SHELBY.

CILLA

I am sorry, Shelby.

SHELBY stops pacing and looks at CILLA.

CILLA

I can say that now and mean it. I wasn't
always sorry, though.

SHELBY

Don't be sorry. Who's to say that I
wouldn't have done the same thing if I were
you? Who's to say I won't someday?

CILLA

What I'm most sorry for is making you feel
that way, that you didn't need anybody. I've
lived my whole life that way, not needing
anyone, never letting anyone get to me. I
was wrong, Shelby. Sometimes what we see
as our strength is really our biggest
weakness.

SHELBY walks over and sits across from
CILLA.

                    CILLA
I can never make up for the life I didn't give
you and I don't expect to be able to make
anything up to you in the time I have left. I
don't even expect you to ever talk to me
again, but please, if you can take anything
from me, take my mistakes. Don't do what I
have done. I don't want you to be dying at
forty-four years old, knowing that not one
person gives a damn that you are. You
deserve so much better than I ever gave you.
Let what I've learned, my mistakes, my life,
be my gift to you.

Both women just sit in calm silence. There
is so much to say, but nowhere to begin and
not near enough time to say what needs to
be said.

                    SHELBY
So what now?

CILLA wipes her eyes.

                    CILLA
I'm going back to Sapelo. Stay with Mama
and Daddy, until it's over.

After a moment, SHELBY speaks.

                    SHELBY
Would you stay with me?

CILLA is surprised, but happy.

                    CILLA
You want me to?

                    SHELBY
Yeah. I do.

SHELBY smiles and so does CILLA.

                    CILLA
I'm kind of tired now. I'd like to go to
sleep, but we can talk all you want
tomorrow.

SHELBY nods.

                                        CUT TO:

INT.---SHELBY'S APARTMENT---
NIGHT.

CILLA sleeps soundly in Shelby's bed.
SHELBY stands in the doorway and
watches her sleep.

                                        CUT TO:

INT.---SHELBY'S APARTMENT---DAY.

SHELBY puts a can of coffee and a mug on the kitchen table. She writes a note on a piece of paper.

INSERT: "Mom,"

SHELBY stops and looks at the word "mom" on the note. She smiles, then continues to write the note.

INSERT: "I picked this up this morning. I have some errands to run. I'll be back in a few hours."

She leans the note against the can of coffee.

CUT TO:

INT.---PAUL'S APARTMENT---DAY.

PAUL is packing his suitcase. The doorbell rings. He goes into the living room and opens the door. It is SHELBY. PAUL smiles and greets her with a kiss, like he always does.

PAUL

Hey, Shelby.

SHELBY

Hey.

PAUL walks back into the bedroom.

146

SHELBY follows him.

PAUL

I'm almost done packing, but I still got to
run to the store to pick up a few things. I
can't believe we leave tomorrow! I can't
wait. Aren't you excited?

When SHELBY doesn't answer, PAUL
notices something is wrong.

PAUL

You're not excited. What's wrong?

SHELBY

My mother came to my apartment yesterday.

PAUL

Your mother? The women you've never
met?

SHELBY

Oh, I've met her. Remember the woman in
my portraits…Aunt Cilla? She's my
mother.

PAUL

Whoa.

SHELBY

You know, I always thought I would be so
angry at her if we ever talked, but I wasn't.
I think at that moment, I was just happy to

finally know the truth. Even today, after I've had time to think about it, I don't really resent her, you know? It is what it is. But, I have so many questions I want to ask her, like why she left? Where she went? Why she never stayed when she would come back? The problem with that is she doesn't have a lot of time left. She's only got a few months to live.

PAUL bows his head, then scratches his forehead.

                    SHELBY
I want to be with her for whatever time she has left.

                    PAUL
So, you're not coming with me.

                    SHELBY
No.

PAUL is upset.

                    PAUL
This woman left you in the hospital the day you were born; she's been in and out of your life without ever acknowledging you ---what kind of person does that to their child, Shelby?

SHELBY

That's what I'm going to find out.

PAUL

And you're going to give up our plans, put
your life on hold for her? I don't
understand.

SHELBY

Neither do I, Paul, but it doesn't matter. I'm
staying with her.

PAUL thinks for a moment.

PAUL

Ok. If that's your decision, then I support
you. (pause) What happens after?

SHELBY

I don't know.

PAUL

What about us?

SHELBY paces around and fidgets with her
ring.

PAUL

Shelby, what about us?

SHELBY

I never expected us to last.

PAUL

Well I do, Shelby. You know you've been
willing things to go wrong for us since the
very beginning---

SHELBY

I have not! I've just been realistic about us!
Nothing good lasts, Paul. Nothing!

PAUL

I love you, Shelby.

SHELBY

Those are just words. Love doesn't mean
anything.

PAUL

Really? I haven't shown you love? That's
bullshit, Shelby! You don't even believe
what you're saying. You're just afraid!
You're afraid because your mother finally
came back into your life, but she can't stay
and you're afraid that I'm going to leave
you too. I'm not leaving!

SHELBY

I told you that's a promise you can't keep!
Let's just end it now before we're too
involved and to hurt---

PAUL

It's too late for that, Shelby. (pause) You
know, it was always easy for you to distance

yourself from your mother, your grandparents, ex-boyfriends, because they didn't care. Well, I'm not going to make this easy for you. I'm going to Paris and I'll be there, waiting for you. And if I have to come home and still wait for you, that's what I'll do. If you come back to me, that's great---that's what I want. But if you don't, just know this---I'm not the one who walked away.

With that, PAUL continues to pack his suitcase. SHELBY just stands and thinks. After a moment, she turns and slowly walks away, seemingly unaffected, a la Daiva.

                                        CUT TO:

EXT.---NEW YORK STREET---DAY.

SHELBY walks to her apartment. She is cool and unaffected, as she walks, yet there is an air of sadness about her.

                                        CUT TO:

INT.---SHELBY'S APARTMENT---DAY.

The door to Shelby's art studio is closed and the lights turned off. SHELBY opens the door, turns on the lights, then walks inside. CILLA is right behind her.

CILLA

Is this your studio?

SHELBY

Sort of. Just a spare room where I draw. I
wanted to show you something.

SHELBY walks over to a shelf that has
fifteen of her scrapbooks on it. She pulls the
first one off of the shelf and hands it to
CILLA.

CILLA

What's this?

SHELBY

Every year, I would make you one of these,
in case maybe you wanted to know about me
and my life. I knew you would come home
about once a year or so. I'd set them out on
the coffee table in the living room. I
thought maybe one day you'd pick one up
and look at it.

CILLA

I never did.

SHELBY

No, you didn't.

CILLA begins to tear up.

SHELBY

I kept making them, though, because I
thought maybe one day you would want to
know about me and my life. My drawings
have always been my way of remembering
things.

CILLA looks through the book with the first
kindergarten drawing, then the drawings of
Palmer and Shelby.

CILLA

How come you never just showed them to
me?

SHELBY

How come you never just looked?

CILLA shakes her head.

CILLA

I don't know.

CILLA sits down and looks through the
book.

SHELBY watches her for a moment, then
leaves the room, closing the door behind
her. CILLA continues to look at the
drawings, spending a lot of time looking at
each one. She stops suddenly when she
comes to a drawing of her and Shelby sitting
on the couch, watching the thunderstorm.

She covers her hand with her mouth, then begins to cry. She studies the drawing, then sobs twenty years worth of tears.

DISSOLVE TO:

MONTAGE SEQUENCE: Cilla's Mistake.

CILLA sits in the living room and looks through another scrapbook.

CILLA and SHELBY sit in the living room and look at a scrapbook together. Shelby explains the drawing to CILLA.

CILLA has fallen asleep on the couch, an open scrapbook spread out on her lap. SHELBY walks into the room and sees her. She carefully closes the book, then covers CILLA with an afghan. She softly touches the afghan and looks at CILLA.

SHELBY and CILLA sit on the couch and talk over a cup of tea and coffee, respectively.

END MONTAGE:

CUT TO:

INT.---SHELBY'S APARTMENT--DAY.

SHELBY sits at her easel and draws.

CILLA comes to the door, knocks, then
enters.

                    SHELBY
Good morning.

                    CILLA
Good morning.

                    SHELBY
You're up early today.

                    CILLA
I couldn't sleep. (pause) I wanted to surprise
you and make you breakfast this morning,
but then I realized, I don't know what you
like.

                    SHELBY
I'm not much of a breakfast person.
Usually, I have a cup of tea and a pastry.

CILLA nods.

                    CILLA
Well, I want to make something for you, so
if you could have anything for breakfast,
what would it be?

SHELBY stops drawing and thinks.

                    SHELBY
Pancakes. I never have pancakes. Grandma

never made them, ever!

CILLA

She never did! She thought there was no
substance to eating a pancake, we always
had to have eggs---

SHELBY

Or oatmeal!

CILLA

Yeah. Never pancakes. Well, Miss Shelby,
that's what I'll make for you. We'll have
pancakes.

SHELBY smiles. CILLA walks out of the
room. SHELBY continues to draw. After a
moment, she hears a crashing sound coming
from the kitchen.

SHELBY

Cilla?

SHELBY gets up and hurries into the
kitchen. She finds CILLA collapsed on the
floor, the pots and pans spilled all around
her.

SHELBY

Mama!

She kneels beside her.

INT.---NEW YORK HOSPITAL---DAY.

CILLA lies in a hospital bed, tubes coming out of her nose and an IV attached to her arm. Her eyes are closed.

In the hallway, outside the door, SHELBY talks with DOCTOR HART. After a moment, she shakes his hand, then walks into the room. She sets her purse down on the table, then pulls a chair up next to the bed. She sits beside CILLA . She pulls the sheets up higher, and straightens them. CILLA opens her eyes. She offers a faint smile. SHELBY smiles back.

                    CILLA
I didn't think the time would come so soon.

SHELBY looks away.

                    SHELBY
Don't talk now, Mama. Save your strength.

                    CILLA
There are so many things left unsaid,
Shelby.

                    SHELBY
Some things are better left unsaid.

CILLA

I have no right to ask you this, Shelby, but please, please...will you stay with me?

SHELBY takes a deep breath.

SHELBY

I'm not going to leave you.

CILLA smiles, and reaches for Shelby's hand. SHELBY grasps Cilla's hand.

CILLA closes her eyes. SHELBY cups her other hand over top of Cilla's and holds on real tight. SHELBY closes her eyes.

FADE TO BLACK:

FADE IN

EXT.---SAPELO CEMETARY---DAY.

SHELBY stands at a gravesite, holding a bouquet of flowers. She kneels down and places the flowers on the grave. It is Percy's grave.

SHELBY

I miss you so much, Perc. I've spent my whole life believing that I didn't need anyone. But, when I lost you, I knew that wasn't true, because I needed you and you were always there when I did. I miss that.

(pause) You know, I always wanted to be you. It wasn't because I was jealous of you and it's not because I wanted anything you had, I just wanted to be you because you were always strong, yet you were open. You just lived and loved and needed...and you were never afraid. (pause) I don't want to be afraid anymore, Perc.

SHELBY smiles at the grave, then gets up and walks away.

                                    CUT TO:

EXT.---YOUNG HOUSE--DAY.

SHELBY pulls up the familiar driveway, SHELBY'S POV.

DAIVA waits for her at the screen door, SHELBY'S POV.

                                    CUT TO:

INT.---YOUNG HOUSE---DAY.

BERNICE and HANSON sit at the kitchen table, still clad in their black funeral clothes.

SHELBY sits on the couch and stares out the front window.

DAIVA is in the kitchen. She pours some coffee into a carafe, then she carries it to the table. Nothing is said.

CUT TO:

EXT.---YOUNG HOUSE---NIGHT.

SHELBY sits on the porch swing. Lightning flashes across the sky.

DAIVA walks out of the house onto the porch, then joins SHELBY.

DAIVA
Are you going to be in Sapelo long?

SHELBY
No. I'm going back to New York tomorrow.

DAIVA nods.

DAIVA
Everything ok there?

SHELBY
Yeah. Everything's fine.

Awkward silence.

DAIVA
I asked her not to tell you.

160

SHELBY looks at DAIVA.

DAIVA
You would have been better off never knowing.

SHELBY looks away.

SHELBY
I always knew. A daughter knows.

DAIVA
Were you with her when…?

SHELBY nods.

SHELBY
I couldn't leave her there alone.

DAIVA nods.

DAIVA
Will you be here for breakfast in the morning?

SHELBY nods.

DAIVA
All right. I'll set a place for you and make your eggs scrambled. You always liked your eggs scrambled with a little pepper and hot sauce, just like your grandfather.

SHELBY smiles.

                    SHELBY
You remembered.

                    DAIVA
A mother doesn't forget.

                    SHELBY
A mother always knows.

DAIVA offers a brief grin, then gets up and
heads for the door. With that, DAIVA goes
back into the house.

A LOUD THUNDER claps and lightning
blazes across the sky.

                                        CUT TO:

EXT.---SAPELO LIGHTHOUSE---NIGHT.

SHELBY stands outside of the lighthouse,
overlooking the marshy pond. She has
Cilla's ashes in an urn. The thunder and the
lightning rage. SHELBY stops and looks up
at the sky.

                    SHELBY
Thunder never scared me anymore after that
night you sat with me.

SHELBY opens the urn, reverently.

                    SHELBY
I shouldn't have waited until now to tell you
that.

SHELBY slowly spreads Cilla's ashes over
the pond, as the thunder and lightning
continue and a harsh rain begins to pour
down. She finally spreads them all and sets
the urn down.

                    SHELBY
Now you can go wherever you want to go.

With that, a huge lightning bolt shoots
across the sky and there is a loud clap of
thunder. SHELBY begins to sob
uncontrollably, years worth of tears that
finally are set free. She kneels on the
ground and sobs.

                    DISSOLVE TO:

INT.---CAB---DAY.

SHELBY sits and stares out the window at
the pouring rain. The cab stops and
SHELBY pays the DRIVER, then steps out
of the cab. She walks into the entryway of
the apartment building.

                                    CUT TO:

INT.---SHELBY'S APARTMENT---DAY.

SHELBY walks around her apartment, absorbing the silence. Three scrapbooks lie scattered around the room, open to various spots. She picks them up one by one. The first one is open to a picture of Percy. SHELBY smiles, then closes it. The second one is open to a picture of Cilla. SHELBY studies it for a long moment, then closes the book. Finally, she picks up the third book. She looks at the grade school drawing of her sitting next to the empty swing. She continues to look at it, while she walks to the couch. She sits down. After a moment, she sets the book down and thinks.

CUT TO:

EXT.---DOWNTOWN STREET----DAY.

SHELBY walks down the street, which is littered with sidewalk cafes. She looks at the PEOPLE sitting at the tables. She stops when she sees who she is looking for.

CUT TO:

EXT.---CAFÉ---DAY.

PAUL sits at a table alone, drinking coffee and reading a newspaper. SHELBY walks up to his table. He looks up from his newspaper and sees SHELBY. He smiles then stands up. She immediately embraces him. They share a long embrace.

                    PAUL
I really love you, Shelby.

                    SHELBY
I know. I know.

They continue to embrace.

MUSIC: Beth Hart's "Stay."

FREEZE FRAME, SHELBY and PAUL.

                              FADE OUT:

About the Author

Kim Damiano wrote her first screenplay when she was sixteen years old. She has always had a passion for writing character driven short stories, plays and screenplays. She was born and raised in a suburb of Cleveland, Ohio. This is her first published screenplay.